Robert William Chambers

A King and a few Dukes

A Romance

Robert William Chambers

A King and a few Dukes
A Romance

ISBN/EAN: 9783743397477

Manufactured in Europe, USA, Canada, Australia, Japa

Cover: Foto ©Andreas Hilbeck / pixelio.de

Manufactured and distributed by brebook publishing software (www.brebook.com)

Robert William Chambers

A King and a few Dukes

CONTENTS.

" Are you going for a soldier, with your curly yellow hair,
And the scarlet coat, instead of the smock you used to wear?
Are you going to drive the foe, as you used to drive the
    plough?
            Are you going for a soldier now ?"

" I am going for a soldier, and my tunic is of red,
And I 'm tired of woman's chatter, and I 'll hear the drum
        instead ;
I 'll break the fighting line, as you broke your plighted vow,
            For I 'm going for a soldier now."

" For a soldier, for a soldier, are you sure that you will go,
To hear the drums a-beating, and to hear the bugles blow ?
I 'll make you sweeter music, for I 'll swear another vow :
            Are you going for a soldier now ?"

" I am going for a soldier, if you 'd twenty vows to make ;
You must get another sweetheart, with another heart to break,
For I 'm sick of lies and women and the harrow and the
    plough,
            And I 'm going for a soldier now."

A KING AND A FEW DUKES

CHAPTER I.

THE FUGITIVES.

SCARCELY had I settled myself comfortably, scarcely had I had a chance to find out what was really in the district, when they came trooping in, tattered, tarnished, grotesque as theatrical supernumeraries, and all atrociously thirsty.

I was sitting on the veranda, cleaning my gun when the weary wanderers entered the valley by the Taxil high-road. I knew who they were at once,—I had been warned that they would in all probability pass my way,—and I was prepared to receive them and make the best of it. I say that I was not entirely taken unprepared but I had not had the faintest idea that they intended to linger longer than over night.   If I had imagined that the King,—but I fear that I am going too fast.   Let me explain a little.

I was sitting, as I say, on my veranda, cleaning the locks of my gun with a fist full of oily rags.   The morning sun blazed in the heavens, sending splendid red lances of light straight through mountain notch over acres of dew-splashed bracken and glistening meadows.

A dainty spring shower had just passed across the valley, vanishing against the northern Caspian peaks in a double rainbow and a light peal of thunder; and I, anxious to be about my business, looked up into the sky for signs of fairer weather.

The signs were favorable.   The ponderous masses of the Caspian Mountains that surrounded the valley on every side were smoking with the rising mists; trees, bracken, pastureland, were ablaze with gemmed dew-drops, and the filmy clouds in the zenith melted into the azure as I looked.

"Good!" I thought complacently, and was on the point of resuming my oily task when something caught my eye—something on the white high-road that winds through the Caspian Mountain notch where it enters the valley. It was a black spot seemingly surmounted by a blinding point of light, and it moved slowly along the high-road in the direction of the Tiflix Valley. I had a premonition of what it was, but to make sure I laid down my gun, went into my bed-room, washed my hands, took the marine glass from my dresser, and walked out to the porch again.

Yes, I was right. There they were, three of them, shuffling along the white highway, and a more despondent band I had never seen.

"They're going across to Austria," thought I to myself, "they won't bother me much I fancy."

I lowered the glass. They were distinctly visible now to the naked eye, three dots on the white ribbon winding up among the rocks into the gorge below the Osman Peak.

The point of light, sparkling and flashing above them, could be but one thing, —the Griffin-crested silver-gilt helmet of the Boznovian Life Guards.

After a moment's thought I went into the house and called Obadiah.

He came from the garden, wiping his hands on his apron, and took off his red skull cap as I motioned him to enter.

"'Diah," said I, "they're coming this time for certain.   There seems to be only three of them ;—I had expected at least a dozen including servants.   I suppose that they left Belgarde rather—er—hurriedly."

Obadiah grinned and rubbed his kinky head.

"You black rascal!" said I, "you've been eating more of those strawberries!"

"Foh Gawd! Mars Steen, ain't nebber tetched no behs—"

"Then see that you don't.   Can you get up a decent dinner for four?   What is there?"

"Sho, Mars Steen ; dah ain't nuffin extra sumptshus to offah de gemmens, sah, but I'se hyah Mars Steen, I'se hyah—"

"And good for nothing except to cook like a Cordon Bleu and loaf the rest of the day," I interrupted. "See that the guests' rooms are aired and do your best with the dinner—and if I find that you have been sampling any more of those seed berries!—"

"Nebber tetched nuffin," said Obadiah.

I went out onto the porch again, discharging my mind of any worry concerning dinner, and sat down on the steps to await the wanderers.

I had not long to wait. Into the valley and down the road they trooped, bedraggled, dusty, thirsty.

The King came first, sweating under his heavy silver helmet, and the two Dukes followed him carrying the common luggage. The King approached the porch where I was sitting and hailed me in the Boznovian language. I answered civilly in French.

"C'est bien!" said the King, entering the garden in that easy unconventional walk of his,—"hey! is this an inn, my good man?"

"By necessity, your Majesty," I replied, controlling my impatience with an effort. I saw that the King had been drinking.

"Then get me something to eat and drink,—ouf!"

He took one of the large wooden chairs on the porch and the Duke of Taxil took another at a nod from the King. The Duke of Babu was wandering around the garden, picking strawberries and devouring them with every symptom of pleasure, and I ventured to remonstrate.

"I am sorry," I said, "those berries are for seed; there are others in the large garden if you care for them."

The Duke of Babu stared at me with his large round eyes and offered no comment, but presently he left the strawberry beds and roamed curiously around the pheasantry where an old cock silver pheasant jabbed at his eyes and then went into a delirium of temper behind the wire sides of his pen.

In a few moments Obadiah appeared ducking and scraping, bearing a tray on which were several crusted bottles of Burgundy and some glasses.

When the King saw Obadiah he laughed outright and spoke to him in the Boznovian tongue.

"He only understands English,—he's an American darkey," I explained.

"Ask him if he'll take service with me," said the King, checking his mirth.

"Obadiah," said I in English, "King Theobald of Boznovia wishes to know whether you will take service with him. And," I added pleasantly, always speaking in English, "if you do I'll break every bone in your worthless hide."

"That settles it!" cried the King in perfectly good English, laughing immoderately," you are a Yankee, mine host, and I'll bet ten thousand marks on it,—hey— I'll bet 'em with you!" turning to the Duke of Babu who only gaped in reply.

"I am sorry—I regret that your Majesty—" I began.

"Nonsense!" said the King, unclasping the chin-guard of his helmet and taking it off, "he's your servant and that's your

own affair.   This wine is pretty good,—
where are you going to put us, landlord?"

"I am not a landlord," I said quietly.

"Have it your own way," said the King;
then draining his glass, "how did you
know that I am the King of Boznovia?"

"Ex-King," observed the Duke of
Taxil sulkily.

"Your Majesty," I said, "the Servian
police notified me that you would probably pass this way into Austria."

"Oh they did, did they," said the King,
swallowing another goblet of Burgundy,
"well they were in a position to prophecy."

"Could you hear the cannon down
here?" asked the Duke of Taxil.   He
seemed to be bitterly ashamed of his com-
panions.

"Yes," I replied pleasantly; "and some
Servian troops, infantry and mountain
artillery, passed through here on their way
to the front.   I supposed the firing was
from the battle of the Genghis Pass."

"It was," said the King, "that's exactly what you heard,—the battle of
Genghis Pass where the Servians played

the mischief generally with me and my army, and—this is the result."

"His own people rose against him," said the Duke of Babu solemnly.

"They had enough of you and Taxil too," said the King, "otherwise you'd never have followed your King into exile."

"The Servians," I ventured, "greatly outnumbered the Boznovians at Genghis Pass I understand—"

"No, both forces were equal in every respect except celerity;—we were quicker in running; and we ran—" sneered the Duke of Taxil.

"Who cares," said the King, "my good brother of Austria will be obliged to support us. I'm glad enough to get out of Boznovia—yes, even thrown out as I was—shoved across the frontier without servants or baggage or horses or fit company or anything but curses—"

"Fit company," remonstrated the Duke of Babu.

"Oh it's good enough for me,—it's the company I kept in Belgarde. I don't wonder that the people revolted after the

Genghis Pass fiasco, and I 'm glad they put that Russian puppet from Marmora in my place.   Russia has got what she wants now and — who cares? — So has Witch Sylvia."

" Perhaps," I observed after a while, "when Austria gets Salonica, you will be given a throne."   I wished he 'd let the wine alone.

" I don't want it," said the King, raising another goblet of Burgundy to his flushed puffy face : " I 'm tired of being shoved and pushed and cuffed and duped by every one of the Powers in turn.   I 'm not subtile,—I have n't an Eastern mind that can expand on lies.   Open another bottle, landlord."

" Russian intrigue is the worst," sighed the Duke of Babu ; " Witch Sylvia is a devil."

"Yes," muttered the Duke of Taxil, " you think you understand and you don't ; you think you see a way to build a railroad and—you don't. Deceptio visus de die in diem."

" I wish," muttered the King, " you 'd

get over your habit of translating into Latin."

Taxil moodily pulled a strand of gold tinsel from his tarnished epaulettes.

"The question is," said the King in a thick voice, reaching for more Burgundy,— "the question is, where are you going to put us, landlord?" He ended in a hiccough.

"Your Majesty," I said, "I object to being called landlord. My name is Stephen Steen of New York City, gentleman of leisure and now here in the Caspian Mountains for my own pleasure. I have rented this valley and parts of the adjacent mountains from the Servian Government as a shooting preserve and trout hatchery. But before the government consented to allow me to experiment with my trout and my pheasants, they stipulated that I should keep my house open as an inn, because it is the only decent house within twenty miles. Therefore, your Majesty, I am ready to carry out my bargain with the Servian Government and entertain you,—but I refuse to receive any compensation, for I choose to regard all travellers as my invited guests."

"Thash all ri'," hiccoughed his Royal Highness, spilling part of a goblet of Burgundy over his uniform in an effort to gulp it down in one swallow,—"thash all ri' my Yankee frien',—we—hic ! we accepsh—we have n't got any money any-way!" and he burst into a maudlin laugh.

The Duke of Taxil looked at me, mortified and furious.

The Duke of Babu, who had been earnestly applying himself to the cognac which Obadiah had brought at his request, tried to appear shocked, failed, swallowed some cognac and peacefully went to sleep in his chair.

"Will you assist his Majesty?" I asked the Duke of Taxil, attempting to repress my disgust.

"No he won't," said the King, rising and wagging his head scornfully.

"Give his Majesty your arm," I said again to Taxil.

"Virtuti non armis fido,—I trust to virtue, not to arms," said the King, and waddled off to bed, ushered by the grinning, ducking Obadiah.

I stood up impatiently and turned to the others.

"Where do I sleep, Mr. Steen?" asked the Duke of Taxil angrily.

I instructed him.

"Come on," he called, roughly arousing the inebriated Duke of Babu, "I'm too tired and you are too drunk to wait for luncheon. It's time this debauch was ended!"

And so their Graces of Taxil and Babu retired to slumber. I preceded them to their rooms and Obadiah pulled off their spurred boots.

The King was already snoring. I heard him.

CHAPTER II.

AN ALARMING PROSPECT.

"THIS," said I to myself, "will not last longer than twenty-four hours." Whereupon I thanked Providence and walked slowly down the stone stairs and out into the pheasantry.

I had been, so far, more than successful with the pheasants, for, whether, it was due to the climate or to my care, the fact remained that I had not lost a single young bird from the pip. Of course there had been a few accidents and mysterious turning up of little toes, but most of these cases could be easily accounted for after a closer investigation.

The birds that had done particularly well were the North American ruffed grouse, the pinnated grouse, the Amherst pheasant, and the silver pheasant.

I obtained a magnificent hybrid of the silver pheasant and the prairie hen, and now I was about to turn a hundred of these beauties into the coverts that stretched from the vineyards to the upper maize fields. All the birds had wintered well, nests were abundant and easily located, and the birds took to the maize and little white wine-grapes as though they had been reared on nothing else. Besides the country was a perfect natural preserve; the long valley, traversed by woods and second growth thickets, was dotted all over with rolling maize fields and vineyards, and it was beautifully sheltered by that southern spur of the great Carpathian range, the Caspian Mountains. As far as the trout went, it was easy work, for the Tschiska, a rapid mountain river, was already teeming with German trout and grayling, and it was a labor of love to build fish-ways above the upper cascades, which opened to trout and grayling four miles of unapproachable water that had, in all probability, never before been stirred by a fishes fins. There were a few otters along the stream but I contented myself with shooting the only two females I saw and letting the dog-otters alone. I hated to shoot any of them but, as I had no otter-hounds nor any desire for that kind of alleged sport, I was obliged to protect my fish. There were also a few herons in the vicinity, but I let them alone, for I believed that there were enough trout in the Tschiska for all of us, now that some of the little lady-otters had been sent to regions where they may hunt and breed for ever and ever in peace.

The valley belonged to the Servian Government. I had a six years lease and an option, at the end of that period, of buying the valley outright. This would also include the slopes of all the mountains facing and surrounding the valley.

The price was not excessive, for the mountains were the stamping grounds for reh-bock and red-deer, and, to my infinite delight, I had seen more than a dozen chamois on the Osman Peak and the three adjacent spurs.

I had, in fact, already decided to buy

the land and make the Tiflix Valley my home for the remainder of my life. Of course it would be an isolated existence,—but what was the world to me? All the joy and warmth and sunshine, had gone out of it, for me, three years before, and for two years I had wandered over a noisy world, seeking some refuge from—what? —a shadow,—a shade that pursued me, that dogged my lightest footstep ;—an echo that never ceased, sounding faintly in my ears as I passed through city street, or woodland path, through wilderness and desert, over oceans, across continents, until I came to the Tiflix Valley, and I thought, perhaps, that here that echo might die out of my ears,—that the shadow might flee away. And I bought the little stone house and I wrote over the door :

" Till the day breaks and the shadows flee away."

Had the shadow fled? As I stood in the fragrant garden I looked on the turf. And I saw the shadow. Had the echo died away? Even as I stood I bent my head to listen, and I heard it, no fainter, no clearer than ever, but always there. It was the echo of a name; for I had loved a woman and she had lied to me.

The vicious old silver pheasant who lived all by himself in magnificent seclusion and undying hope that he might one day peck my eyes out, now began to bow and bob and strut and scratch gravel, which were always the preliminaries to his working himself into a passion. Then he began that harsh short screaming, ending in a series of metallic clucks which sounded like two stones knocked together. "You old devil!" I thought, "now you'll begin to hiss. Of course Obadiah must be somewhere in sight." Surely enough the wicked old bird scratched more gravel, pirouetted once or twice and hissed venomously. I turned and looked about me. Seated at an open window, palm-leaf fan in hand, lolled Obadiah. It was the window belonging to the room where King Theobald of Boznovia lay asleep. Obadiah was softly talking to himself. He neither saw me nor heeded the rage of the pheasant, and I crept up to the house wall under the window and listened.

"Gwuff'm hyah, fly!" muttered Obadiah, waving his fan, "doan, yo' persoom to obnoxiate de sof' snuffles of de high 'n' mighty,—doan' you do it! Gwuff'm hyah, 'skeeter! 'Diah 's gwine swat yo' ef yo' doan' git. De high 'n' mighty King ob de ebber-lastin' gole an' diamon' palace am a sleepin' an' a slumberin' an' a snufflin' like he gwine bus',—bang!—he head off!" The pheasant across the garden was fairly squealing with rage. Obadiah heeded him not.

"Ole 'Diah gwine run away wif de high 'n' mighty King—he! he!—ole 'Diah he gwine git!"

I reached up and grasped Obadiah by the back of the neck.

—"And no more stolen strawberries, eh, 'Diah? Come out of that you shiftless roustabout or—"

"Foh Gawd! Mars' Steen, did n't say nuff'n—leg go mah wool!—"

"Come out of that!" I said firmly

and I lifted the treacherous darkey clean out of the window, and down among the poppies at my feet where he rolled his eyes appealingly, opened his mouth once or twice and collapsed.

"Now," said I, " if I catch you trying to sneak off after the King of Boznovia when he goes away to-morrow, it will be the worse for you ! What do you mean by attempting to leave me in the lurch in such a place as this ? Answer ! You good for nothing ungrateful glutton,—who is to cook for me if you go ! Do you think I 'm going to put up with a Servian or a Roumanian, or a Bulgarian, or a Turcoman ? Are your wages not doubled and paid a year in advance ? Get a move on you, quick."

Obadiah was stricken with contrition and in palliation of his contemplated flight he pleaded that he was dazzled by the nearness of so much royalty, and that he had been seduced by the careless offer of the King. The words "gole an' jools an' precious stones," "sumptohus high 'n' mighty," and " miss'ble sinner," were so much mixed and mumbled that I cut short his apology, accepted it, and bade him go about his business which was to finish weeding the lily bed.

"Some day," said I, "a wandering Kurd or Cossack will catch you and stick knives all over you if you run away from me."

Obadiah's eyes rolled but he said nothing.

"And," I continued, moving away, "if the Kurds don't catch you one of those big Carpathian bears will and he'll pull all the kinks out of your wool and shell your body out of your skin as a man shells a pea-nut."

This affected Obadiah so profoundly that I was obliged to assure him that there was no immediate danger of bears; but it was half an hour before Obadiah resumed his normal smile, which measured six inches across.

I walked through the garden, now all abloom with great spicy Turkish roses, crossed the high-road, and threw myself down on the grass.

For a while I lay there idly, touching the grass with indolent caress, moving my fingers among the pebbles and tiny clods of moist earth. Then sitting upright I patted the solid sod as a potter pats his clay, thinking; "If I had made it all, how different I might have made it!" And I stooped swiftly to the earth and inhaled the incense from the grass and the soil, and dug little holes with my fingers, watching the movements of the ants and the minute field insects, with curious eyes. The grass brushed my chin; the little creatures of the field hurried hither and thither, startled, perhaps by the great eyes fixed on them from above, yet each busily working out its fate,—each following its appointed destiny.

"It is all good," said I, thinking of the greater eyes that watched me as I was watching; "it is all good; it is good to live and be alive and lie on the bosom of the world." I tapped upon the earth with my finger tips.

"Underneath lies the balm," I said; "I press upon it with my breast and it shall heal this heart of mine even as God heals my soul."

I lay heavily, my head between my flattened hands, my mouth against the earth. For there is a mystery in the fragrant aromatic crust of the globe that is only solved when the soft flesh of human lips press it, whispering their secrets.

After a time I lifted my face, looking long and thoughtfully across the tops of the meadow-weeds to the solid mountains, towering pinnacle on pinnacle into the blue. Then brushing the sweet earth from lip and chin I sat up in the sunshine.

"Who could die," thought I, "with a broken heart, when the earth and the scented grass are here to heal?"

An eagle was hanging high in the zenith, moving imperceptibly southward in a straight line. A gnat floating above my nose looked larger.

"It depends," said I to myself, "on the point of view. There is much to live for;" and I lighted a cigarette and jumped up.

The Duke of Taxil was staring at me from the porch.

"Good afternoon," said I, "did you sleep well?"

"I've been ringing and ringing," said the Duke, "because I want a siphon of seltzer." He placed his hand upon the back of his head as he spoke.

His Grace of Taxil was feeling the Burgundy.

I went across the road, through the garden, and called Obadiah.

"Get the club-soda and the cognac," I said ; and, turning to the Duke ; "the sun is very powerful to-day ; it seems to me,—if I may venture to suggest,—that the bear-skin dragoon's busby you wear is a little heavy for the season."

"It's the head-gear of my regiment," he answered sulkily.

When the brandy and soda was brought he swallowed it in silence, raising his eyes piously and placing one hand upon his bosom as the glass was slowly inverted.

"Um! A—h!" said his Grace of Taxil, "I fancy I did it justice ;—fiat Justitia, ruat cœlum you know,—I 'll have another."

" Est modus in rebus," said I, " one will cure your headache, two will double it."

" You are right my friend ;—I did n't know you spoke Latin."

" I don't," said I,—" I know enough to say that, but that 's nothing, and you know, ex nihilo nihil fit. Is his Majesty still asleep ? "

After a moment the Duke of Taxil wiped his beard with his handkerchief and muttered something about " a fool of a King."

" It has been a great honor to meet you all," I replied, for I saw that he felt the disgrace keenly.

" You probably never would have met us had we not sunk to this," said the Duke, with that innate tact peculiar alike to Boznovian and British noblemen.

" True," said I cheerfully, " until I came here I never heard of Boznovia."

The Duke of course took this as a confession of culpable ignorance.

" Education in the United States is not

compulsory I believe," he said, pouring out another brandy and soda and blinking his puffy eyes. "It's different with us."

"Rem acu tetigisti," I replied smiling, "it's different with you."

"Now what the devil does that mean?" said the Duke.

"Oh it's Latin," said I, "a mere matter of education you know."

At this juncture the King arrived, heavy eyed, rumpled and shockingly thirsty. I ordered more brandy and soda.

"I'll go no further to-night," growled the King, eyeing his Grace of Taxil malevolently. He was still drunk, but, under his mask of ostentatious inebriation, I fancied I could detect a deeper current of bitterness and humiliation.

"I trust I shall have the honor of your Majesty's company to night," I said.

"Oh you will," sneered the Duke, "and you'll probably have it for the rest of the week."

"Why not?" demanded the King; "I'm tired and this is a good inn,—good enough for a drunken outcast, eh, Taxil?"

"But," I began—

"I say it's a good inn," repeated the King; "I'm not particularly anxious to see the Emperor of Austria. He'll probably be disagreeable, won't he, Taxil?"

"You expect to stay a week?" I asked desperately.

"Probably," said the King, "unless you turn me away."

"Perhaps a month," suggested the Duke maliciously.

—"Or two," added the King.

"This," said I, "is not an inn—"

"It's good enough for me," said the King, sniffing the odour from the kitchen where Obadiah was broiling trout.

"For me, too," said Taxil, "and if it's good enough for us it's good enough for Babu."

"How do you suppose that I am going to provide three or four meals a day for five people?" I demanded.

"Oh," said the King vaguely, "Babu does n't eat much; he's in his cups most of the time. That leaves meals for only four."

"And your negro,—he need n't eat much ;—that makes meals for only three," said Taxil with a bitter smile.

"Do you eat a great deal ?" suggested the King looking at me.

"I eat what I need," I replied, intensely annoyed.

"Well, well," said the King, "don't put yourself out for us ;—if you tell me where the cellar is, Babu will bring us what wine we need."   He laughed weakly but I saw his hand tremble.

"I don't see," I said, "how your Majesty can be comfortable in my house without proper clothing and toilet necessaries.   You can't go about the country with a heavy silver helmet on your head ; —his Grace of Taxil can't be comfortable in that fur busby and gold-slashed uniform,—his Grace of Babu will be wretched if he goes around wearing his admiral's uniform and cocked hat—"

"It 's not an admiral's uniform," said the King, "it 's a vice-admiral's uniform."

"I beg your pardon," said I.   The Boznovian navy consisted of one despatch boat on an inland body of water with no outlet to the ocean. I did not see the necessity for such accuracy. "I beg your pardon," I repeated, "I only intended to demonstrate that your Majesty would be more comfortable in Austria."

"Oh we have some baggage with us," replied the King, carelessly; "Babu and Taxil brought toilet articles and that sort of thing. Can you lend me a shooting cap?"

"I also should be glad of a hat," observed Taxil.

"Your King will be served first," said his Majesty, with a drunken laugh, and reached for my shooting cap which was lying on the chair beside me. I declined the offer of his helmet and paced the piazza moodily until Babu came out carrying half a dozen of my hats, a straw relic of London, a wide-awake from Sofia, a crush hat from Paris, and several shooting and fishing caps, one or two bristling with trout-flies. Taxil appropriated a straw hat at once, while Babu crammed the wide-awake over his ears and gaped at the King.   It was all like some hideous opera bouffe.

" Help yourselves, gentlemen," said I, contemptuously.

The King noted my tone.

" That is true," he said, " we have n't left you anything except shooting caps, but I 'll send you a dozen from Vienna, if I don't die of alcoholism before I get there."

At that instant Obadiah announced dinner and we all trooped in, the King first, Babu and Taxil following and squabbling about something or other,—and I bringing up the rear.

They cleaned that table to the last crumb!   Each demanded a whole bottle of claret for himself,—I was wasting no more Burgundy,—and they smoked my cigars and they guzzled my cognac and Scotch whiskey until I thought that if this was to be repeated every day, my ruin was merely a matter of time.

The King was in good spirits, but he was fearfully intoxicated.   He rallied Taxil on the disgraceful flight of the cavalry and taunted Babu with the unheroic conduct of the sailors at the Genghis Pass. Taxil replied hotly, but Babu, already stupefied with wine, regarded the King with an apathetic stare.

The King brushed the crumbs and wine splotches from the front of his uniform where rows of little orders and medals tinkled with every movement. He offered to decorate me with the order of the Blue Griffin, "for," said he, "no cook in Belgarde ever prepared such trout or such sauce."

I declined, observing that I was not a culinary expert and had no ambition to receive the Cordon Bleu.

"Not Cordon Bleu,—Blue Griffin," explained his Majesty ; "don't you want it, landlord ? "

"I have requested your Majesty not to call me landlord," I said shortly ; "give the Blue Griffin to Obadiah if you wish to decorate a cook."

So the King gravely unfastened the jewelled order, beckoned to Obadiah, and placed it in his shaking hand. This completely destroyed the tottering equilibrium of the darkey's mind.   He imagined himself something or other by the Grace of God and he walked with a sort of prance as though he were leading armies and all the bands were playing " Hail Obadiah !" That night too, he looted the hot-house melon vines, and I took it out of his hide next morning, which reality brought him back to earth.

" I don't object to you wearing the Blue Griffin," I said, " but you are to understand that it's a cook's decoration and carries neither patent of nobility nor any special dispensation to rifle my melon vines.   I think you comprehend this now, do you not ? "

Obadiah caressed the seat of his trousers.

" Go," said I, " and see that the ' sumpt-shus King' is not nosing about for the cellar keys.   If I miss a single bottle that has not been sent for by me, I 'll hold you responsible.   Go !' "

Obadiah left hurriedly, rolling his eyes.

I had set that day aside for a few hours' trout fishing along the upper reaches of the Tschiska. I also intended to build a little on one of the sheltering break-waters which I was constructing to secure calm water and gravel for spawning beds. So I had my luncheon with me, a pint of Rhenish and a bit of cold fowl, and I also took a light brush fowling-piece, for foxes had been worrying the birds lately, and I had no mercy on them.

As I passed the porch the King answered my greeting very civilly and asked where I was going. I told him. He must have gotten the impression that I was going trout fishing solely in order to supply him and Taxil and Babu with their favorite delicacy, for he suggested a net as a valuable instrument for securing a mass of food with the minimum of toil. I explained. Then he wanted to go fishing himself and pointed at the rods lying in a corner of the porch, but I discouraged his project as best I could, for I had no intention of turning the monarch loose on my carefully cherished preserves.

Taxil, who sat under the fig trees, whispering to Babu, looked up and intimated that it might be agreeable to shoot a few pheasants for a change.

"Of course," said I scornfully, "you know the season is close and the hens have chickens ?"

"What of it," said Taxil, "game out of season goes well."

I sçowled.   These pheasants had cost me on an average, five pounds apiece so far and the experiment was only beginning. So I scowled at Taxil and walked to the edge of the lawn.

"It is impossible," I said without ceremony ; "luncheon, tea, and dinner will be ready when you order them.   My servant is under your Majesty's orders;" and I walked away toward the forest.

Before I reached the rocky path that leads across to the swift flowing Tschiska, I could hear, far behind, the King, bawling for Obadiah and brandy.   I was not nervous ; I had left a certain amount of liquor in the butler's pantry, but the cellar keys were in my own pocket.

"Let him bawl," said I to myself.

CHAPTER III.

A VOICE IN THE FOREST.

I WALKED on through the noble fir forest, puffing my pipe and looking out for any stray grouse or pheasant, for I loved to watch my birds as a shepherd watches his flock. The pheasants rarely came into the fir woods; the grouse did sometimes come but seldom stayed. There was one game bird, however, that seemed to fancy the firs, and of this bird I saw a fair number as I strolled along, smoking my pipe and sniffing the balsam saturated air. It was one of my experiments, this game bird,—a cross between the prairie chicken and the domestic Guinea fowl. And it proved a wonderful success, lying close to a dog, flushing in perfect form, wintering well, and feeding on berries and maize until almost too plump to fly. It had none of the maddening tricks of the Guinea fowl either, so I was more than satisfied, as I watched these heavy, strong winged birds, whirr up from the thickets and go spinning down the dim wooded forest aisles. ·

And as I walked I thought of the King as I had left him, heavy jawed, leaden eyed, bawling for brandy. I knew his history,—most people know it I dare say. Suddenly hustled from his little independent Duchy of Taximbourg by Austria and Germany, he had been thrust, despite the menacing growl of Russia, upon the vacant throne of Boznovia. Theobald of Taximbourg came from a sodden unintelligent line of Princes noted chiefly for their intemperance and poverty.

From the crusading junketings of the early Theobalds, his ancestors had been noted for the freedom with which they supplied themselves with heirs, and the bar-sinistre played the important part in their quarterings, to the physical and mental detriment of the Taximbourgs. It told too in their professional pastimes, for all of the Taximbourgs were better blacksmiths, clock-menders, gardeners, and carpenters, than they were Princes.

The present King, it was rumored, was the offspring of a Taximbourg and a complacent circus-rider. There may have been no truth in it, for the King cut a sorry figure on horseback and bon chien chasse de race.

He made a bad mess of it on the Boznovian throne, although his aunt de facto, the Dowager Duchess von Schwiggle, worked like a Trojan, stormed like a griffin, and, as some ill natured people added, swore like a pirate to keep him there. But what can an old lady, although she be a Dowager, a Duchess, and a von Schwiggle, do against the insidious machinations of that vast hell of intrigue called Russia? First of all came the Russo-Afghan trouble, which at one moment brought England and Russia face to face. British lion and Russian bear leered at each other and snarled for a week, but the time had not yet come, and the death clinch was postponed. But in that brief week, King Theobald of Boznovia gave himself away by entertaining the British Minister at an extraordinary banquet, and Russia never forgot it. Then came the Servian-Bulgarian war, and King Theobald, instead of minding his business, interfered and brought all the Balkan states about his ears, buzzing like infuriated wasps. Servia never forgot that either, so when the time came, and Russia gave the signal, Servia fell upon Boznovia and played the mischief with King Theobald. The campaign had been ludicrously brief—a few weeks' skirmishing and the fiasco at the Genghis Pass had aided the Russian secret agents in Belgarde, and when King Theobald rushed madly from the Genghis Pass to his capital of Belgarde, he found a frenzied populace enthusiastically waiting to run him out of town and across the frontier. And while they were about it they evidently decided to make a clean sweep, for they hustled the corrupt Duke of Taxil and his bibulous Grace of Babu over the frontier to keep the King company, and advised them for their skin's sake, to point their noses toward Austria and follow them diligently.

The Austrian Emperor was furious, partly because his protegé had been mauled, partly because he knew that now he should have to support him. He uttered terrible threats and ostentatiously mobilized two army corps. But he got small encouragement from the Triple Alliance, for Italy openly jeered him and the German Emperor was too busy composing an opera, to bother about Boznovia.

That settled King Theobald, and, after a half hearted attempt to drag Bulgaria to his rescue, he gave it up, gathered up his bundles, and started for the Austrian frontier.

Poor fellow! The Servian police had warned me that he might pass my way, but I never expected to see him so utterly destitute and without servants or baggage. "Those Balkan people can be as savage as any Turk when they make up their minds," I thought, remembering Major Panitza and Stambouloff.

And as I walked, my gun swinging lightly from my shoulders, my gaiters scraping the ivy crowned thickets, showering my shoes with fragrant dew, I felt a tenderness, a deep pity for these outcasts who had taken possession of my house, and I determined to let them enjoy themselves as they pleased.

"What 's a trout or two?" I argued; "the King may take my rod if he likes; I 'll tell him so. But I draw the line on netting trout,—and on slaughtering breeding pheasants. I 'll just give him a chance at the Guinea grouse if that will amuse him. Yes, and I 'll let him shoot red-deer and chamois if he cares to,—and he may have a try at a Carpathian bear too."

So I walked on, pitying the lot of the tramp King, deciding to give their Graces of Babu and Taxil my cellar keys and let them drink themselves to death if they pleased. And all the while I kept my eyes open for the Guinea grouse, and my ears open for the quhit ! quhit ! quhit !-t-t ! whir-r ! of the rising game.

The fir woods had given place to more

open groves of walnut, chestnut, and linden ; the ivy grew thicker among the
roots and underbrush, and broad patches
of sunny ferns and brake clustered along
the path now cut by a mountain torrent,
now by a carrefour, deserted and partly
overgrown.

On the soft loam along the spring brooks'
bank I saw the tiny heart-shaped print of
the red-deer and the broader impression
of the stag. A wild-boar too had been
that way, a sow, I took it, followed close
by her little fierce long bristled piggies.
Once, passing a salt lick, I saw the human-
like mark of a bear's foot, and, a little
further on, a dozen perfect imprints where
a wild-cat had marched around in a bit of
swampy ground and had sharpened his
nails on a young tchozza tree.

"A tom-cat," I mused, "preparing a
serenade for Mrs. Pussie to-night. They 'll
probably dine on one of my grouse."

When at last I came to the Tschiska
River, I unstrapped my gun, flung my
creel and rod on the moss, and sat down
to wipe the perspiration from neck and

chin.   Then I bathed head and face and wrists in the sweet icy stream, drinking long deep draughts, spirting the water from my mouth like a triton at play, burrowing luxuriously into the silvery bottom sands with both hands, until the little trout fry along the bank scuttled far and near in dire dismay.

A Russian sable peered cunningly at me from a cleft in the rocks, wrinkled its nose, sniffed, and withdrew hurriedly.   A great white alpine butterfly with brick red spots on its wings, fluttered about me fearlessly, finally alighting on one of my wet shoes.   I watched it uncoil its proboscis and begin a capricious luncheon from the moisture glistening on my gaiters.   The wood-flies and saw-flies filled the dim woods with their buzzing ; jewelled spiders wove in the sun, watching for gnats, or scuttled in and out among the galleries of their gossamer labyrinths.   Somewhere near by, a thrifty wood-mouse was busy among the beetles in a rotten log, and, high above the pines on the cliffs, I heard the squealing of young kestrels.

"The world," said I to myself, "is very beautiful and kind," and I bit a piece from the wing of a tender fowl, washing it down with a swallow of Rhenish. I ate leisurely, often pausing to watch the bullet-like flight of some big stag-beetle, or the felonious efforts of the small field mouse to abstract my bread from the paper parcel near me. Bottle in one hand, bread in the other, I listened to the melody of bird music and the music of the brook bubbling over pebbly pools, and I smelled the fresh smell of earth and leaf and water, until my heart was full of tenderness for everything. So I gave the mouse the rest of my bread.

A few rods below me, jutting straight out into the stream, was a small break-water that I had begun. It was designed to secure a still deep backwater, gradually shallowing toward the foot of the pool, where the trout could spawn in peace among the gravel and pebbles of the bottom.

When I had eaten my luncheon I washed my face and hands and went down to the half finished dam.   Under the bank I found my cement and trowel, and very quickly I mixed some water-proof cement, picked out a dozen stones of the proper shape and size, and began to work, whistling softly.

The little fishes swam up to the rock where I stood, goggling their big round eyes, opening and shutting their mouths as if in amazement.

" Public improvements," said I, glancing at them ; " it's all for your benefit my friends."

A grayling, its splendid dorsal fin cutting the water, its iridescent sides a-glitter, sailed solemnly past, turned at a sound from me, and disappeared like a streak of pearl-colored flame.

" Bonne chance ! " I laughed, " you will weigh two pounds by August ! "

A school of tiny trout had already congregated in the quiet pool below the break-water, and there they lay in ranks, motionless save for an almost imperceptible swelling and relaxing of the spotted gills.

" They 'll grow," thought I, " so here 's health to them ! " and I scooped up a cupful of water from the pool and drank it ; whereat the little trout turned tail and fled.

I used up what cement I had prepared ; the break-water had grown a little higher and longer ; so I tucked my tools away in their hiding place beneath the bank, rinsed my hands, and went back to get my rod for a cast or two in the larger pools above.

These pools were a quarter of a mile up stream. There was a disused wood-road, which ran along the opposite bank of the Tschiska, connecting ten miles through the forest with the Taxil high-road ; so I picked up my rod and landing net, slung my light fowling-piece over my shoulder, and, crossing the Tschiska on the rocks, struck into the wood-road, whistling merrily.

" What a fool I should have been," thought I, " to have gone into the army and lived the dog's life of a gentleman ranker, just because the most beautiful woman on earth broke my heart."

Overhead a big raven croaked approval. I looked up, and, as I looked, another raven winged its way across my path, and then another and yet more, "all croaking approval," I thought to myself, watching the last one flapping by.

Six ravens! And the old rhyme rang in my ears:

> "One is a warning,
>   Two are mirth,
>   Three in the morning
>   Bring Death to Earth.
>   Four ravens flying
>   Announce a birth;
>   Ravens five bring sorrow anew,
>   Six black ravens,—a bride for you."

"A bride!" I laughed grimly, "where is she, O raven prophets?" And I looked around with an ugly sneer.

Hark! From somewhere in the forest came a sound, distant, vague, now clearer, now indistinct. And now again it came, faint but unmistakable, a human voice, a dull halloo, quavering, dying away in the wilderness. At the sound of that far cry my heart stood still, then beat furiously, leaping up and setting all my pulses bounding ; for, in my breast the echo of a voice, long silent, had responded in spite of me.   And I looked at my feet and I saw the shadow of the past floating upon the ground.

" Because," said I furiously, "some lost fool is calling for help in the woods, I forsooth must hear in that voice the tones of *her* voice !   Is this to go on ?   Am I always going to gape and shake when a strange voice is raised in the world ? Why in God's name can't I learn to forget !"

And I sullenly unslung my gun and fired both barrels.

CHAPTER IV.

THE DUCHESS TAKES A DRIVE.

SCARCELY had the crashing echoes of my shots died out among the trees when an answering hail came back, the heavy hail of a man's voice, and I flung my gun across my shoulder and hastened forward along the wood-road.

As I pressed on, the hails became more frequent and intelligible, the voice of a man bellowing in the language I most detest,—German; and I answered cheeringly as I passed lightly through the forest.

"Idiot," I thought to myself, "as far as I can make out he 's in the wood-road itself. Why does n't he come to meet me?" Then, as I rounded a curve of the road, I caught a glimpse of a horse's head, and, in a moment more I came in sight of a strange group.

A big closed carriage, old fashioned and shabby, stood wedged among the trees of a wind-fall.   On the ground, in front of the horses' heads, sat a red faced old gentleman, flourishing and vainly attempting to fire a horse-pistol.   He was also bellowing at the top of his lungs. When he saw me he stopped bellowing, cast his pistol angrily into the road, and began to talk German very fast.

"Stop!" said I pleasantly but firmly; "I speak English and French and some Italian."

At the sound of my voice another man thrust his head from the curtained carriage window and ejaculated; "Herr Je!"

"You are mistaken," said I, settling my cap and wiping my forehead, "my name is Steen.   If you can talk English talk it."   Then, looking more narrowly at the head thrust from the carriage window, I saw that it was not a man's head after all, but the forbidding countenance of a woman—a regular grenadier of a woman. I removed my cap in some confusion and murmured, " Pardon madame."

The fat red-faced old gentleman who had been eyeing me in amazement now waddled up and placed his mouth close to my ear.

"That," said he, "is the Dowager Duchess von Schwiggle!"

"I thought," said I, whispering in my turn close to his ear, "that it was a trooper of the body guard. Will you assure Madame the Duchess of my devotion and beg her to dispose of my services?"

We had been talking in French. If I spoke it as badly as he did, purgatory should be my portion.

"General!" cried the Dowager Duchess.

The fat man waddled hurriedly to the carriage window. After a few moments whispered consultation, during which both the Duchess and the General cast stealthy glances at me, the General again came over to where I stood.

"I am General Bombwitz, Chief of Staff of the Boznovian army," he said, puffing his mottled cheeks into demi-balloons. "Come with me,—you are to

be honored by a presentation to the
Duchess."

"This," said I, "is too much honor,—
it is indeed!"

"Compose yourself," said the General.

"I am no coward," said I, "sound the
charge!"

"Young sir," said the Duchess, speaking in French that echoed through my
head like the roar of a drill-sergeant, "on
you we count to extricate us from this
forest."

"Ah," I murmured, "you are lost then,
Madame la Duchesse?"

"Lost!" repeated the Duchess in that
remarkable booming voice, "Herr Je!"

"It was the Servian's fault," said General Bombwitz gloomily; "he told us to
take this wood-road."

"Where is the Servian?" snapped the
Duchess.

"Fled," replied General Bombwitz;
"he ran away when he saw that you were
annoyed."

"And he knew his business," thought
I, adding aloud; "doubtless Madame the

Duchess was on her way to Belgarde. The Taxil high-road will take one to——"

"I was not on my way to Belgarde," said the Duchess, darting a suspicious glance at me. Then, without asking pardon, she and Bombwitz began another whispered conference which lasted long enough to weary me, so I sat down on a log and examined my gun.

Presently the Duchess called to me and I rose and walked up to the carriage window. Then I noticed for the first time that there were two other women in the carriage, but before I could see them distinctly in the half light of the drawn shades, the Duchess spoke again, demanding my name.

"Stephen Steen," I answered pleasantly.

There was a movement in the carriage, —a dog yelped as though suddenly hustled, and the Duchess frowned and cast a terrible glance over her shoulder.

"Who stepped on Mops?" she hissed. Silence.

Then she turned to me again. "What sort of a name is that?" she asked.

"Which,—Mops?"

"Certainly not!" said the Duchess furiously,—"your own!"

"Madame," said I, "it is an honorable name."

"You keep an inn, do you not," demanded the Duchess.

"My home," said I, "but I doubt that my present guests are in a position to make my fortune as an inn-keeper."

"Who are your present guests," asked Bombwitz with a cautious nod to the Duchess.

"Oh a King and a few Dukes," I replied carelessly.

There was an interval of strained silence. I thought I heard a sound from the interior of the carriage,—a quickly suppressed snicker; I may have been mistaken.

The Duchess and the General were beginning the series of preliminary nods and coughs which threatened another whispered consultation, but I stopped it short.

"What is the use of all that?" I said to General Bombwitz. "If the Dowager Duchess von Schwiggle is on her way to see her nephew, the King of Boznovia, I

can direct her in a moment.   I 'm no spy
nor do I care tuppence about any of the
Balkan squabbles, but I would like to go
trout-fishing if you have nothing to ask
of me.   If you have, ask it."

I was not mistaken,—I did hear a
snicker this time, but the Duchess suppressed whatever sound it was, and General Bombwitz puffed and hemmed and
walked around in little circles like a
pigeon.

"Inn-keeper,"—began the Duchess.

"Madame," I interrupted, "my name
is Steen, and I am no more of an inn-
keeper than General Bombwitz here.   If
you wish to see his Majesty you are very
welcome to stay at my shooting box !"

"He 's an American," murmured the
General to the Duchess, "he 's probably
mad, as they all are."

"I 'm not afraid of a mad inn-keeper,"
said the Duchess with that evil sneer peculiar to some Germans, and she turned
insolently to me again.

"Which is the best road to your inn,"
she demanded.

" Madame," said I with my most careful bow, "all roads lead to Rome, but
there is only one that leads to my home,
—the road of common courtesy.   Permit
me to set you upon that road " ; and before either Bombwitz or the Duchess
knew what I was about, I took the horses'
heads, backed the carriage, lead it through
the trees and around the windfall, into the
wood-road again.

" Jump in," said I to the General who
came puffing and floundering through the
brush after me, " it is not far but the
road is hard on little fat legs ;" and I
gently propelled him into the carriage in
spite of himself.   I took the horses' heads
again, settled my gun on my shoulders,
and started on.   Behind me I could hear
an excited discussion carried on in whis-
pers, broken now and then by a smothered laugh or a shriek from the trodden
lap dog.   Then the Duchess' head was
thrust again from the window.

I looked back, smiling affably into her
stony perplexed face.

" It is a great honor, Madame," said I,

"to be able to render the wohl-geboren Duchess von Schwiggle this little unimportant service. 'We of the new world esteem it a privilege to learn from the old world those little courtesies and attentions of which we know so little. Ah ! la delicatesse ! il faut la chercher en Allemagne, Madame la Duchesse."

The face of the Duchess was a perfect blank. Once or twice she opened her thin lips as though to speak, but nothing came of it, and her heavy countenance relapsed into its normal granite immobility.

When we came to the ford at the crossing, I waded into the Tschiska, encouraging the horses and letting them drink,—a thing that the Germans behind had probably never troubled themselves about during the entire journey. Poor brutes, they plunged their soft dusty noses into the stream and sucked and gurgled and drew deep draughts of the sweet water into their parched throats. I started to wash their heads and chests a little and the Duchess' head emerged from the carriage again.

"What is the delay?" she asked.

"Ordinary humanity," I replied shortly.

"We are pressed," said the Duchess, tightening her thin lips.

I went on bathing the horses.

When I was ready I led the horses safely across the Tschiska, up the bank and into the wood-road again. Then I sprang into the driver's seat, gathered up the reins, and we trotted away at a livelier pace, the road permitting it on this side of the Tschiska.

Several times the Duchess and the General opened opposite windows and bawled at me, but I paid no more attention to them and drove as I pleased, letting the horses take it easy when they chose.

At last we turned into the Taxil highroad about two miles above my home and the horses moved along at a good pace, for it was all down hill and the road was a military road.   As we came in sight of the white stone house and the gardens all blooming with great Turkish roses, acacias, fig-trees, and flowering almonds, I felt something of that delightful sensa-

tion of home-coming which all exiles yearn
for.

Yes indeed, I had decided that this
white house, tucked away in the Caspian
range, should be my home ; and my days
of wandering were to be over at last.
North, south, east, west, the ponderous
Caspian mountains towered, blue with
the afternoon haze upon their flanks, and
I heard the west wind soughing through
the firs and the whistle of martins in the
sky.   The white dust rose along the
flashing wheels, the jingle of bit and chain
sounded pleasantly in the summer air, and
I bent from my seat, calling the horses
pet names and talking the talk that good
horses love to hear ; for I was happy for
the first time in years, and the voice in
my ears and the shadow at my feet had
vanished.

So we sped up to the cool white house
where the lindens drooped and the silver-
pheasant was calling ; and I read above
my door the words I had written there a
year before :   " Till the day breaks and
the shadows flee away."

"Had they fled?" I asked my heart, as I drew rein and the Duchess and the General tumbled out. And my joyous heart beat : "They have fled away."

"Come," said the Duchess grimly, peering into the carriage.

A maid in a cap alighted, bearing the wretched lap-dog, Mops, and then—and then !—

A great dizziness seized me; I felt as though the whole world had slipped from under me, for there,—there, descending from the carriage, smiling, dainty, self possessed, was the woman I had loved, Marjory Grey !

I heard my own voice saying, "Madge, Madge !" but I did not know I spoke aloud.

She turned deliberately and looked me straight in the face. "Thank you Mr. Steen for your very great kindness," she said with a daring smile, and in a moment had slipped away to join the Duchess who was making much of the King on the porch.

His Majesty had appeared, hearing the

sound of wheels, but he was not exactly dressed for a reception. The Duke of Taxil had been shaving him—he was unable to do it for himself—and now he stood there in his shirt sleeves, half lathered, stanching a razor-cut with one hand and waving a towel with the other, while the Duchess encircled him in her vigorous arms and embraced him enthusiastically on his shaven cheek.

His Grace of Taxil, a mug of lather in one hand, was hob-nobbing with General Bombwitz while the Duke of Babu, stupefied with liquor, gaped at everybody, including Mops and the maid.

Marjory Grey looked about her, but said nothing.

I was past all speech.

CHAPTER V.

IN THE ROSE GARDEN.

THE sun had not yet pushed its crimson disk above the grey flanks of the Osman Peak, but I was already out, clothed from head to foot in a warm soft leather shooting suit; for the summer mornings in the Caspians are chilly, and the great dewdrops on leaf and blossom tremble and splash like pools of quicksilver.

Pushing through the garden where the scented roses slapped my face, soaking cap and coat, I turned by the pheasantry, not heeding the insults of the old silver pheasant, and came to the abode of Obadiah. He was already up, grumbling and shuffling about, and I rapped on the window to summon him.

"'Diah," said I when he appeared, "what meat have we in the ice-house?

There must be the better part of the last stag and enough mutton from Tiflix to last until Constantine comes."

"Yessah," said Obadiah slowly, "an' bofe de red-bucks—" he meant reh-bock, —"an' de shammy am a hangin' an' a frizzin' on de ice."

"Good; what winter vegetables have you?"

"'Taters, sah, squash an' turnips an' sass in de garding, sah."

"Well," said I, "you must attend to all that.   I 'll see to the horses ;—those Germans would never bother their heads. Come, hurry,—you can pin on your Blue Griffin decoration after dinner.   Remember we have seven guests now, not counting me.   And—er—'Diah, you can take —er—special pains with Miss Grey's dinner."

"Yessah."

"And you need n't attempt to do the rooms,—the Duchess' maid will attend to Miss Grey as well as to the Duchess, and the King will have to do his own chamber work."

"Yessah,—an de dooks sah?"

"The Dukes can go to the devil!" I muttered; "has Georgiades driven up with the milk this morning? Oh he has, eh! And did you tell him to bring it for eight to-morrow? Good, you do know something, 'Diah, don't you?"

"Yessah," said Obadiah, casting a sly glance at my face.

"Then prove it," I said cheerily, and walked through the garden to the house again.

When I reached the porch I sank into a chair leaning my head on my hands. I was deadly tired, but my fatigue came not only from having tossed through a sleepless night but also from another reason,—despair.

The amazing apparition of Marjory Grey in the Tiflix Valley,—here at my very door, had utterly crushed me. All the evening I moved about like a man in a trance, hearing my own voice as I gave orders or answered questions, presiding at table, attending to the wants of the hungry Boznovian nobility through the medium of Obadiah, but neither in voice nor action, nor gesture recognizing myself, so shocked and dazed was I.

And at last they had all gone to bed, the Duchess and Marjory Grey attended by the maid, the King to his chamber where he presently fell asleep and snored so heavily that the Duke of Taxil rapped furiously on the floor with the pommel of his sabre and I heard him protesting at intervals through the long night.

I did not sleep ; I lay tossing among the crumpled sheets, and my face was now hot now cold as the blood surged or ebbed with my thoughts. For I was beginning to realize what had happened,—I was beginning to understand what it meant to me.

That Marjory Grey should be in company with the Dowager Duchess von Schwiggle did not astonish me when I reasoned it out, although the last that I had seen or heard of Marjory was in Bar Harbor, Maine.

Marjory's father, a brilliant officer and a widower, had taken service with the

Khedive of Egypt, in company with half a dozen other clever American officers who saw a chance for legitimate advancement in their profession. It was perhaps due to Admiral Hobart Pasha's influence with the Khedive that his younger friend Colonel Grey became Grey Pasha of the Egyptian Staff and finally Military Attaché of the Egyptian Embassy to Berlin. It was in the Prussian capitol that Grey Pasha saw and loved and eloped with Hilda von Raupenhelm.

The small earthquake that shook Germany when the news spread, threatened to bring on international complications, until the Dowager Duchess von Schwiggle, fascinated by the audacity of Grey Pasha, declared that she would leave the couple all her money and her clumsy schloss at Lauterschnapps unless they were forgiven and received. This tickled Bismark who patched up a peace; and Grey Pasha took his pretty wife back to Cairo and cabled his daughter to leave her convent school in Montreal and come to Cairo.

5

I remember very well the day I told Madge I loved her.   It was during Christmas week.   She was spending it as usual with her aunt in New York, and I, as usual, was at the house every day and all day and as late in the evening as I dared.

She had been very sweet to me, in fact she had consented to write to her father about me in May when she was to leave the convent forever.   I hardly know now what it was that came between us,—a shadow that at first I refused to recognize. But the shadow crept in ; I became anxious, then wretched, and finally, when she came again at Easter, I spoke.

At first she only laughed at me, but after a while I saw that her impatience and even displeasure were no longer miserable fancies of mine and I began to believe that she not only never had loved but that she was incapable of loving.   I was mistaken.   I learned my mistake when young Hamilton of the artillery spent his month's leave at Bar Harbor that summer.

I suppose I acted like a fool,—most

men do when their hearts break.   Madge
and I were walking along the shore; she
had just received the cable, and her aunt
was going to Cairo with her.   She was
full of the excitement of going; it was
perhaps a bad time to reproach her.
That evening was her last at Bar Harbor
and I asked her to save it for me.   She
told me that she had promised Hamilton.
In the ten minutes that followed I—God
knows how!—stamped out the last smould-
ering spark of tenderness that might have
been left between us.   That was the end.
A moment later Hamilton and her aunt
came and led her away.   She went without one word or glance.

In the months that followed I heard of
her occasionally, now in London, presented at court, now in Berlin, chaperoned
by the old dragon von Schwiggle, now in
Cairo for the winter.

Rumor had her engaged to marry the
young Earl of Drumgilt, the Baron von
Allerdings, the brilliant Comte de l'Oise;
and after a while, when young Hamilton
resigned and followed her to Cairo, the

papers said it was a settled affair and printed columns of spread-eagle bunkum and twisted the lion's tail until I could bear no more and I wandered away to find some place where newspapers and rumors were unknown.

It was two years before I believed that I had found that place, here in the Caspian mountains. And when at last I was sure that I had found it I wrote above my door: "Till the day breaks and the shadows flee away"; and sat down to battle with my misery.

A year had passed and yesterday I told myself that I had forgotten;—yesterday I was happy for the first time in all those years, but to-day!—At the thought I sat up and stared at the fiery edge of the sun, now peering above the mountains beyond the Notch.

Overhead the sky was drenched with crimson; the dappled clouds absorbed the splendid dye and clustered along the vast vault of heaven like drops of blood. Flecks and shreds of fire streamed from horizon to horizon; the mountain tops burned with a deeper hue. As yet the chilly pastures, dim in the shadows of the mountain wall, sparkled grey and pale under their lifting sheets of fog, but, as I looked with sick eyes on the fair fresh world, the meadow mist drifted away in tattered ribbons, the gemmed grass glimmered, sparkled, then flashed out a million rainbow rays, and the little meadow pool rippled, tinted with amethyst and pearl.

Everywhere birds were singing, from pasture and vineyard, from maize-field and forest, thrushes, linnets, finches, hedge-sparrows, twittering swallows, sky-larks, caroling among the clouds. From the orchard came the scream of a rosy-breasted jay and the husky note of a magpie ; in the woods a cuckoo called and called until the whole forest was full of echoes and the valley rang with the fluty notes.

A drowsy bee stumbled from its bed in the heart of a rose and clung buzzing to the edge of a leaf, drying its dewy wings. A great moth crept into a spot of sunshine and sat, its brilliant wings a-quiver.

In the house a door opened and shut ;

I heard steps on the stairs, a shuffle across the lower floor, then suddenly a startling crash as though a hundred tin pans had been kicked across the hallway.

I sprang to my feet and looked into the house.   It was the King.

"My confounded helmet," he said peevishly, "fell off;—I was coming down for a drink,—the bell wire is broken in my room."

He stood in the hall, enveloped in an ermine edged robe, a sputtering candle in one hand, a beer-mug in the other. His big silver helmet lay on the tiles near the door.   I suppose he had put it on for warmth.

"The beer is in the butler's pantry is n't it?" he said sleepily.

"I 'll get it," said I ; "be careful! your dressing gown is all spotted with candle wax !"

"Dressing gown !" yawned the King, "it 's my coronation robe; I have n't a dressing gown to my back.   I 've got another head and an up-to-date taste in my mouth."

I said; " Do you want some seltzer ? "

" No! no!   A litre of Munich beer is what I need.   I 'm sorry to trouble you ; I could n't sleep,—Taxil snores so—"

He gaped, coughed, picked up his helmet and sat down on the stairs.

" I 'm sorry to trouble you," he repeated ; " if you like I 'll get it myself. I 'd better begin to learn to do a few things for myself I suppose.   I may have to stay with you indefinitely."

" I beg your pardon ? " I faltered.

" I 'm sorry for you Mr. Steen but do you know what my aunt the Duchess has come to tell me?   Why just this : my good brother of Austria can't receive me because Russia insists that I go to England and says there 'll be war if I don't. Now I 'm damned if I go to England, so there you are.   Please do get me my beer."

I drew the homeless King into the dining-room where there was a fire and called to Obadiah to bring a litre of beer.

" Now," said I firmly, " let us discuss this thing.   Do you mean to say Russia insists upon your leaving Europe ? "

"Yes she does," said the King.

"Can't you go to Taximbourg?"

"No, Russia won't let me."

"What about France then?"

"What Russia says, goes in France, my friend. It's no use, I have gone over all the map of Europe and the complications that would ensue are enough to make my hair come out. I'd go to America if I didn't hate the ocean so. Ah, here's the beer!"

He dipped his mottled nose into the mug and slowly drained the quart measure to the last drop.

"Another," he said, blinking at Obabiah, "and then I'll go back to bed."

"Your Majesty," said I, "it will be difficult for me to keep you here if Russia objects. If the Russian spies don't know you are here, the Servian Government will inform them and you will be obliged to leave sooner or later anyway."

"Then what am I to do?" asked the poor King.

I was touched. There really seemed to be no spot in the world for him.

"I don't know," I said. "Believe me I am very willing to try to keep you here, but you could not live in comfort in such a place. I should think you'd rather go to England—"

"Have you ever been in England?" asked the King.

"I? Oh, yes—"

"Then why do you suggest it?"

"Why?" I repeated, smiling.

"It's gloomy!" said the King sulkily. "I'd prefer the Fortress of Peter and Paul! No, I'll be hanged if I leave the Balkans. I don't want to be King any more; my tastes are simple as the devil. Plain clothes, plain food, plenty of Burgundy and Munich beer, and a sunny corner to doze in, that's all I want on earth. It isn't much, is it?"

"No," said I, "it isn't much."

"My confounded aunt the Duchess von Schwiggle, put me up to all this regal fol-de-rol. I've no stomach for a kingdom and less stomach for fighting to keep it. My stomach and digestion are not good anyway. Well, prosit!"—drinking deeply—" I don't find I can hold any more liquid with a crown on my head than with a straw hat.   The Duchess can say what she pleases.   I 'm going to live incognito and that settles it.   Thank you for your trouble, Mr. Steen, I 'm going to bed and I don't want to be called for breakfast."

I watched his Majesty shuffle away and mount the stairs, gathering his gold brocaded coronation robe around his bare legs, but I felt more like weeping than like laughing.

By this time the sun's rays had chased the misty chill from the air ; the big silver pheasant was screaming in the garden and the bantam rooster answered him from the stable.

Lina, the blue-eyed maid of the Duchess von Schwiggle, peeped over the banisters and presently tripped down to carry up coffee for two.   Obadiah took some chocolate and toast to General Bombwitz, but when he knocked on the Duke of Taxil's door he was anathematized.   Babu, on the other hand, was too drunk to reply, so I bade Obadiah let their Graces alone and attend to the kitchen.

"The maid will help you," said I ; "these people must know that one servant can't do everything. Don't take any orders from the Duchess, do you hear ? I am able to direct this outfit."

"Yessah ; de Duchess doan' bodder 'Diah 'n' 'Diah ain' gwine bodder de Duchess."

"All the same if she makes any suggestions about reh-braten, you need n't despise them," I said, picking up my shooting cap and opening the door.

"Doan' 'spise nuffin, sah," sniffed Obadiah ; "h 'it am de po' an' sinful dat 'spise."

"True," said I, lingering ; "you can take special pains about Miss Grey's dinner. Miss Grey is very fond of strawberries. I have a suspicion that there are more ripe ones under the leaves in the new bed."

"Whaffoh you 'spicion dat, Mars Steen ?" enquired Obadiah.

"Because," said I, "you always leave the new bed when you see me. We will have no more of that sort of thing now."

"Yessah," said Obadiah cheerfully; and I went out, closing the front door behind me.

As I walked toward the stable the turkeys craned their necks, uttering liquid gobbles, the hens followed, clustering and crowding about my feet, and stray long-shanked pullets rushed headlong from distant corners to join the whole clucking feathered mass. Several old hens hurried up, conducting their downy peeping broods, the ducks waddled from the meadow pools, the geese arrived, necks stretched, fat white bodies rolling in unison.

I stirred the feed in the porcelain platters, mixing in the corn and mottled beans, and set it down close to my feet. It is very pleasant to feel the eager press of warm feathered creatures about your legs. Close contact with helpless living things makes a man a bit more considerate I imagine.

At length the horses were fed, the

bantam rooster had achieved the last of a series of victories over all comers, and the water-fowl were solemnly pursuing their pigeon-toed course toward the meadow pool again. One or two reluctant hens still lingered, pensively picking at the polished platters, the downy chickens hovering near, plaintively peeping.

I stepped into the gun room and looked at the glittering row of fowling-pieces, rifles, and rods, hesitating, touching first one rod, then another.

" No, I 'll not fish," I thought, " I 'll just stroll a bit and see what the birds are about ;" and I lighted my pipe, dug my hands into my shooting-coat pockets, and sauntered toward the road.

As I turned past the porch the door opened and Marjory Grey stepped out. She did not see me at first ; she was sniffing the rose-scented air, nose tilted, eyes fixed on the mountain tops.

My heart was beating fast but I strolled into view and said pleasantly ; " Good morning Madge ; I hope you slept well."

She started when she heard my voice ;

it was a bit sudden I know,—after all those long years.

I viewed with equanimity the swift color in her face; I was quietly pleased that I had taken her unawares and that she had betrayed it.

However she answered immediately, without the slightest trace of embarrassment; "Good morning Sten,"—her old name for me,—"and, thank you, I slept beautifully."

" And the Duchess?" I enquired, perfectly at ease,—outwardly, I mean.

" The Duchess has gone to sleep again; she was very much fatigued. May I come down into your delightful rose garden?"

"Come," I replied pleasantly, "will you wear a belt-knot of Turkish roses, Madge?"

"But,—oh thank you,—but you must pick them; see, here is a beauty, and this, —and these two half blown buds—oh dear! it is too difficult to choose :—choose for me, Sten."

It might have been a week instead of

three years ago since we had last met. We walked along, side by side, I cutting the stems of the dew-soaked buds with my sheath-knife, she examining the garden, stables, house, and pheasantry with curious wide eyes.

"Is your father well,—and your charming step-mother of whom I have heard so much?" I asked.

"Papa and Mamma are very well; they are spending a few weeks on the Bosphorus. Papa often asks about you—"

She stopped rather suddenly.

"Well?" I enquired.

"I have not been able to tell him very much," she resumed placidly, "but now I shall have lots to tell. Are you well?" she added.

"I? Oh yes. And you, Madge? but your face answers my question—"

"Does it? I am three years older."

"Three years?" I asked hypocritically, —"not three, Madge—"

"Why yes," she insisted turning toward me, "have you really forgotten that—"

"What?"

" Nothing,—if you have forgotten."

" Please don't think I have forgotten anything," I exclaimed earnestly ; "the long vacations when you wore your hair in two braids, the long absences when you went to the convent,—and later too, when you left the convent, I remember our boy-and-girl love affairs,—ah Madge, we were very serious then—"

" Really," she said, surprised, " do you call those boy-and-girl love affairs ! "

" Don't you ? " I asked, mastering my voice with an effort.

" I ? I was seventeen and you were twenty ! Why if I had imagined that you took it so lightly—"

" Not lightly, Madge," I said, " I was quite upset when you gave me my congé, —I was miserable—for nearly a week ! "

" A week ! " She looked at me half angrily, half curiously.

" Oh more than that," I said,—" it must have been more, for I remember now that I lost the July trout fishing because I be-lieved that my life had been blighted. Poor Hamilton,—how I hated him for a month or so."   I was smiling at her now but the smile on her lips was not as genuine as it might have been.   And I lost nothing,—the flutter of an eyelid, the beat of the pulse in her soft throat, now whitening, now faintly deepening in color as her wonder changed to impatience.

"You were right too," I continued gaily ; "suppose that I had not come to see,— as you did,—that we never really loved ? Suppose I had never gotten over it,—that I had borne the wretchedness and hopeless misery always,—always with me, night and day, sleeping, waking ?—I tell you, Madge, it was a fortunate thing that I found out that I also had never really loved ! Would you like to see my pheasants ?"

"Pheasants ?" she repeated, standing still in the path,—"oh yes,—if you wish."

The old silver pheasant was in a tantrum as usual, and promptly flew at my eyes as soon as I touched his wire barriers.

"A perfect old scold !" I laughed ; "I only keep him as a warning to myself. Is n't he a beauty, Madge ?"

"Yes."

6

"There are some golden pheasants in that further enclosure,—there !—you can see one of them now. They are not hardy enough to turn out, but I am very much interested in cross breeding—"

"You seem to find everything interesting," she interrupted with a peculiar smile. "I, on the contrary, find most things very uninteresting."

"I beg your pardon, Madge," I laughed ; "I might have known you would n't care for this sort of thing—"

"Tell me about yourself," she said, slowly moving on.

"About myself ?   Why there 's nothing much to tell. I am very contented and happy, I have n't a care in the world or a wish ungratified. I fish and shoot and build dams and breed pheasants."

"Oh !"

"Besides, I have my fruit ;—there are strawberries here, — you were fond of strawberries, Madge, were you not ?—or was it—".

"Who ?" she said impatiently ; "of course I was fond of strawberries. I wish,

Sten, that you would arrange the reminiscences of your salad days more methodically."

" I beg your pardon, Madge,—"

" You need n't,—and you are not at all flattering." She looked at me again, curiously. "You have changed very much," she said.

We had strolled back to the house as we spoke and now I halted as though to take my leave.

"You will find everything that I have to offer at your disposal,—except servants," I said. " I am sorry but perhaps you can manage with Obadiah and the pretty maid,—what is her name?"

" Lina," said Madge shortly.

" The house is yours," I continued smiling, " I shall not trouble you much for I am out poking about the woods most of the day—"

" Sten," she said, " have you no curiosity to know how I happened to come here?"

" Why yes," I replied, " you must tell me all about it some day—"

" I shall not tell you at all!"

" Please do, Madge," I laughed.

"I shall not," she retorted, half smiling, half angry,   "you evidently don't care tuppence to know and you are not a bit cordial."

" Listen," I said seriously, " I do mean to be cordial ; you know I am glad to see you once more—"

" Once more !   Sten, you are absolutely so self-satisfied—"

" No, only self-sufficient—"

"— It 's the same thing !"

" Pardon me, Madge, the first is imbecility, the last is merely sanity."

She sat down on the edge of the piazza and pulled at the leaves on the rose bushes.

" I don't know you,—I feel that somehow you are very different," she said ; " I am conscious that you are utterly changed in every way ;—are you ?"

" How ?" I wondered that I could so control my voice.

"How? Oh, how do I know ? You were always very impulsive and warmhearted, and—oh I don't know. Your face has changed too—"

"Well, yes," I laughed; "I am thinner and more bronzed, and these lines show a little more deeply, I suppose."

"What did they come from?" she asked, looking straight at me.

"Age," I said gaily.

"No suffering?"

"Not very much. I of course loved a woman as is the fate of all men. She was not very enthusiastic over me and of course it hurt for a while. I doubt that it deepened these lines very much."

"She did not love you?"

I shook my head, smiling.

"Was she young?"

"Rather young."

"Pretty?"

"Oh yes."

"Good?"

"Very;—much too good for me, Madge; —you have cut your finger on the rose thorns—"

"I know,—was she young—I mean pretty—no, I mean was she—oh Sten, tell me about her!"

I laughed outright. "There is nothing to relate. I was fascinated of course, —I might as well tell you that I really did love her,—the first woman that I had ever loved,—and the last. That is all."

" Oh," said Madge, " it is fortunate for me that we found we did not—"

" Love ? Oh that, of course, was salad love—"

She colored furiously and stood up.

" It was very real to me," she said haughtily ; " I am amazed—"

" Madge," I interrupted, " please don't think that I hold that valueless. No indeed,—it enabled me to distinguish between love and friendship—between infatuation and love. You taught me to think, when I only believed you were cruel and selfish—"

" Did you believe that ?"

" Yes. When you went away with Hamilton I could have killed myself. I often wondered why you were so merciless that night."

" I have often wondered too," she said.

" But you told me you loved Hamilton."

"Did I ? I don't know why I said so."

"Did n't you love Hamilton ?"

" No."

"Who then—pardon me, Madge, I—"

" I don't mind your asking ; I loved nobody—then. I did care more for you than anybody else."

"It 's very sweet of you to say so," I said laughing.

"It is true. But you are right, Sten, I loved nobody ; I was inexperienced, too young, too excited over the prospect of going abroad, to love. A young convent girl is the most emotionless thing in the world in some ways."

What I wanted to ask was ; "Where is Hamilton ?" What I did ask was ; " Do you keep up your singing ?"

"Singing ?" she repeated, "oh yes, I sing. Do you remember how you always asked for that aria from ' Carmen ' ?"

"Yes," I answered, giving the impression that I had really forgotten. It hurt me more than it did her.

"Tell me," I blurted out at last, unable to keep up the bitter game, "tell me about all those rumors.   Are you going to marry Drumgilt or the Count d'Oise or anybody ?"

She gave me one quick glance, then something came into her face that I recognized,—something that I had seen before, long ago in those years when she knew that I loved her.

" Fool !" I thought, "idiot that I am ! She knows it now !"   And I turned on her in desperation saying something stupid to give her the idea that I was indifferent and heart-whole,—that I was far beyond her power for working me weal or woe.   It was too late,—I saw it in her eyes, in the droop of her red lips, I saw it in the poise of her slender figure ; and I knew that she knew.   .

" I am going," said I, rising, "to look after my young pheasants.   I don't suppose you would care to come ;—the Duchess, you know, being alone—"

" I understand," she said sweetly, " I will go to the Duchess."

CHAPTER VI.

A COUNCIL OF WAR.

I RETURNED at noon after a sulky tour through the coverts, furious to think how I had played into Madge's hands,—mortified that she should have read me so easily.

"I 'll show her that she 's mistaken," I muttered, "only let me have a chance !"

There was nobody in sight about the house except Lina, the blue-eyed maid, and Mops, the over-fed lap-dog. The one was escorting the other.

"Lina," said I, "where is her Grace the Duchess ? "

Lina dropped me a pretty curtsey.

"Excelenz," she replied, "her Grace the Dowager Duchess von Schwiggle and the high-born Mees Grey are attending a council of war which was called by the

illustrious General Bombwitz on behalf
of his Majesty the King."

"Oh," said I, "and the Dukes?"

"Their Graces of Taxil and Babu are
also present," said Lina.   At this juncture
Mops took offence at my hob-nailed shoot-
ing-boots and approached them, growling.

"Doubtless a German dog," I said.

"Yes sir."

Mops drew in his breath, gurgling dis-
approbation.

"Does he bite, Lina," I asked.

"Oh I hope not sir!" she said
timidly; "come here Mops!"

The wretched poodle suddenly snarled
and snapped at my legs.   Lina uttered a
soft shriek.

"Perhaps," said I, "you had better pull
him away, Lina—see! he has hold of my
leather gaiters.   If I should touch him it
might be that I should yield to an inclination and send the Duchess into crêpe.
Does black become the Duchess, Lina?"

By this time Lina had removed and
slapped the venomous Mops.

"Excelenz will pardon the annoyance,"

she stammered,—" Mops shall be whipped by me—"

" No, no," I said, "the dog did no harm,—he only chewed off a button."

" If permitted I will willingly sew it on for his Excellence—"

" Thank you, Lina, with pleasure. By the way, call me Mr. Steen,—if you can say it you know—"

" Meester Stin," said Lina shyly. She was as dainty a little creature as was ever turned out of a Dresden china shop.

" Thank you," said I, noticing how prettily her hands were fashioned. She was just now fingering her lace edged apron.

" Do you think," said I, looking carefully around the rose garden, "do you think, Lina, that there is any unpardonable sin in a kiss?"

" They say so," said Lina, examining her pointed shoes.

" And do you believe it?"

" Yes."

" Then," said I determinedly, "it is time that somebody exposed such an absurd doctrine." And I kissed her in the interest of civilization. Having done this conscientiously, I did it again in the interest of common sense. Mops growled. Lina looked at Mops.

"Now," said I, "we have performed a duty that we had no right to shrink from. Lina, I am going to the Council of War."

"They are in the dining-room, Mr. Steen," said Lina, looking at me sideways!

"Ha!" said I to myself, fiercely, "that shows how little I am to be swayed by any influence of Madge Grey. She has played her last game of battle-dore with my heart!" And I entered the house and knocked at the dining-room door. The Duke of Taxil opened it.

On seeing me the Dowager Duchess von Schwiggle frowned and whispered to the King, but that monarch shrugged his shoulders impatiently and called out to me to enter.

"You are welcome, my friend!" he cried heartily, "come in and instil a little common sense into this company. Nobody knows anything except Miss Grey—"

" Theobald !" exclaimed the Duchess, horrified.

" It 's true ; don't tell me ! I know what I 'm saying. Come, Mr. Steen, we want your advice."

"I am very willing," said I, quietly seating myself beside Madge.

" The case is just this," began the King ; " you see that Russia—don't interrupt me, Bombwitz ! I was saying that Russia is determined to pack me off to England and I won't go and there you are !"

" Why," said I, " should Russia wish to exile you ?"

" Because I know too much about some things. I could set all the Balkans in a blaze if I chose to take the trouble—"

" You should choose !" boomed the voice of the Dowager Duchess.

" Now, now !" said the King, " my good aunt, you can't get me to go into any more filibustering expeditions, for I won't go and that settles it. I 'm not ambitious,

I 'm no King by inclination,—I 'd rather be a decent clock-maker than a fool King. I won't be a King !"

"You must !" boomed the Duchess, her face hard as granite. Taxil seconded her, Babu yawned, and General Bombwitz puffed out his cheeks, assuring everybody that his brains and his sword were at the King's service. Madge Grey looked at me.

" Do you want to be King again ?" I asked.

" No !" shouted the King angrily.

"Yes ! Yes !" cried Taxil and the Duchess.

"If you want to be King," I said, " it would be easy for you to enlist the King of Caucasia and you 'd have the whole Caucasian nation to back you. All you 've got to do is to promise them free entry into the Balkan Sea for their commerce and their navy of two torpedo boats."

The Duchess stared at me, open mouthed ; General Bombwitz was speechless, and the Duke of Taxil sank helplessly into his big arm-chair.

" It seems to me," said Madge Grey,

her eyes sparkling, "that Mr. Steen has thought of the one thing that might restore his Majesty his throne."

"It is strange," said the Duchess, "that it took an American to think of this."

"It is strange," said Madge solemnly.

"But it's colossal! splendid! glorious! prachtvol! wunder-schön!" exclaimed Bombwitz.

"In another moment I should have probably thought of it myself," observed Taxil.

"I also," added Babu in a thick voice.

"Don't you see," I explained, "once you enter Boznovia at the head of the Caucasian army, Servia will back down, and Russia's policy is always passive when it concerns the Balkan states. She may not recognize you as King, but she won't dethrone you by force,—at least not outwardly, for if she does, Austria, Bulgaria, Roumania, Caucasia, and Boznovia will ally themselves with England—"

"Confound it all!" cried the unhappy King, "I don't care a copper pfenning what they do! I won't be a King! I won't I won't! I—"

"You shall!" boomed the Duchess.

"You must!" echoed Taxil and Bombwitz. Babu was asleep. Madge Grey looked at me.

"Don't you understand!" wailed the King, "suppose we all did get back into Boznovia; how are we to stay there? Who's got the brains to keep us there? We can't always have Mr. Steen to explain the difference between chalk and cheese to our addled brains!"

"Why not?" said Madge Grey, "you could make him Prime Minister." A spot of scarlet was burning on each cheek. Her eyes were very bright.

At this astounding proposal the Duchess started and glared at us. Bombwitz blew out his cheeks until they seemed on the point of exploding, and Taxil laughed sneeringly.

"By Heaven! I'll do it!" said the King; "I tell you I'll do it if you force me to this business. I warn you all,— yes, you too, my excellent aunt,—as surely

as I decorate him now for his common
sense,—" here he suddenly turned and
threw over my head the chain of the first
class order of Saint Theobald,—"I will
raise him to the highest place in the
kingdom!"

Then the King stood up and turned
sharply to Taxil.

"It is through such finance jugglers as
you," he said haughtily,—" and such imbecile peers as his Grace of Babu, that I
goaded the people to revolt. Who was
it counselled me to invite the British Am-
bassador to the Palace when Russia was
sniffing at the gates of India? You!
Who was it that urged me to interfere
when Bulgaria was thrashing Servia?
You, and you too, General Bombwitz.
And neither of you thought of anything
except reward and plunder ;—you, Taxil,
expected to feather your nest, and you,
Bombwitz, intended to appropriate a field
marshall's baton and perquisites. If I
were a King at heart instead of a good
natured, slow country gentleman, I should
have sent you both to the Black Fortress

and I should have had his imbecile Grace of Babu made cellar steward in the Palace. As for you, my good aunt," continued the King,—and now as he spoke he really began to look like a King,—"as for you, I should have courteously conducted you to your schloss of Lauterschnapps and bade you stay there in God's name and keeping."

For a full minute there was absolute silence.

Then the King said; "I am a quiet simple man, not gifted with much good sense and slow to think, lax and overfond of comfort and peace, and I say to you that it is wrong to urge such a man on to war,—to urge such a man to crown himself again. I am not a bad man,—but I am worse than a bad King,—I am a stupid one."

He turned to me.

"Mr. Steen, is it not the truth?"

"Yes, your Majesty," I answered.

He held out his hand with a gesture so helpless, so utterly sad, that I bent low and took it humbly. Then straightening up I said; "if you want my services they are yours, in field or in council, whenever and wherever you wish. It would be better for you and for Boznovia if you never went back, but, if I were you—" here I struck the table with my clenched fist— "I would never rest until I returned and showed the Boznovian people, for my own pride's sake, that when I chose I could be a King for any country to honor!"

"Bravo!" cried Madge Grey, and clapped her little white hands.

"Am I to go?" said the King turning almost fiercely on the Duchess.

She nodded, a little dazed.

"Then Heaven have mercy on you, Taxil, on you, Bombwitz, and on that useless hulk, Babu; for I will reign like a King and a just King, and I will show no mercy to thieves or cowards or imbeciles! I will go! Madame, my good aunt, permit me to conduct you; Mr. Steen, I claim your aid. Stand by me now for, as I live, I will show you what a King can be!"

CHAPTER VII.

IT was two o'clock in the afternoon.
His Grace of Babu was sleeping a
vinous sleep under the linden in the pasture opposite the house. Taxil sat on
the edge of the duck-pond, gloomily fishing for dace with a rod that he had un-
earthed in the stables. When a fish bit
he jerked it bodily out of the water onto
the grass and fell upon it. This at last
awoke the inebriate unter den Linden,
and he watched the bouncing flapping
fish with every symptom of terror until,
satisfied that they were fish and not multi-
colored snakes, he turned over and prepared to doze again.

The King had decided to call another
council of war and the Duchess suggested
that we all walk through the woods to

some pleasant nook near the Tschiska, suitable alike for weighty consultation and for Mops to take a bath.

So at two o'clock when the shadows on the mountains were beginning to lengthen toward the east and all the fields were vibrating with rhythmical crickets' rune, we started; Madge Grey, the Duchess, the King, Bombwitz, Lina, Mops, and myself.

As we passed the duck-pond, I hailed Taxil and Babu, and they reluctantly obeyed, plodding sullenly across the pasture. The strident rattle of grass-hoppers and the tic! tic! tic! of the locusts among the maize stalks seemed to intensify the heat of a nearly vertical sun.

A fine dusty powder greyed the fern-leaves that bordered the road ; the field flowers drooped a little, waiting for the evening dew. Brilliant active tiger-beetles ran hither and thither across the baked soil, or rose on burnished wings and sailed away down the road ahead of us, only to fly up again as we overtook them.

The Duchess walked ahead majestically, followed by Lina and Mops. The

King came next, rambling along in his easy, unconventional way, talking with Madge Grey. Since this morning's outburst there certainly had come something into the King's carriage that gave him an air of being somebody. Perhaps it would be going too far to call it dignity or even authority. Still, whatever it was, it was noticeable, nay, unmistakable. Bombwitz and Taxil felt it, I could see that, and the sodden Duke of Babu recognized it. Madge perceived it, I know, for I caught her eye once or twice. Whether the Duchess or Mops were aware of it I could not determine.

The Duke of Taxil, still lugging his rod and string of dace, exhaled an irritating aroma, and the Duchess told him so without hesitation. So he laid his fish down in the grass to pick up on his return, but Mops waddled toward them, sniffed them, and began to roll on them uttering amused yelps.

"That may be fun for the dog, but it won't improve their flavor!" cried Taxil angrily.

"Dace are not good to eat at this season of the year," I said.

"I eat what I choose," said Taxil sulkily.

"Hello," I thought, "Taxil is beginning to be jealous of me."

We now turned away from the highroad and entered the woods by a footpath, thick with dead leaves, crossed by slender budding vines, and doubly criscrossed with shining strands of spider's gossamer. The Duchess broke a dozen spider's webs with her granitic face and then ordered Babu to go ahead and perform that duty for her. Babu went: it was all the same to him what he hit with his nose, for the only sensation left in his alcoholic skin was the sensation of inebriation.

Mops waddled along like a true German, noticing nothing that other dogs would have noticed, passing all sorts of holes and logs and thickets and interesting smells without turning his stupid head. I hate such a dog. Men who are not manly, women who are not womanly, dogs who are not doggy, inspire me with resentment.

"He is like all those globe-trotting Germans who never look at anything but are simply bitten with a mania to swarm over countries and walk as far as possible," I thought to myself. I looked at Bombwitz. There was an uncanny facial resemblance between him and Mops.

"General Bombwitz," I whispered, "has our friend ever been a parent?"

"Herr Je!" gasped Bombwitz, "her Grace is unmarried!"

"Her Grace!" said I, "why I was speaking of Mops."

Bombwitz puffed out his cheeks, coughed twice, and waddled on.

I laughed a little and joined Madge Grey.

"Madge," said I, "let us stop saying what we don't mean and meaning what we don't say. Shall we,—for a change?"

"Hush," she said, "the Duchess will hear you. What do you mean?"

"What I say—this time. May I walk with you a little? Shall we drop behind, —so the Duchess won't hear?"

She stood aside with a charming gesture, bidding Taxil and Babu to pass ahead. Then, as they lumbered by, she fell into the path again and I stepped up beside her.

"Of course you know," said I without any preliminary warning, "that I still love you."

"Sten!" she exclaimed.

"I thought we were going to be truthful for ten minutes," I said.

She was silent.

"After the ten minutes are over," I continued, "we will fib away as merrily as ever; it would be too stupid otherwise—"

"Flippancy does not become you," she said with heightened color.

"I 'm sorry. I feel flippant when I watch the insincerity of my friends."

"Do you mean me?" she asked slowly.

"No, Madge. You are not insincere."

"À la bonheur alors!" she laughed. Her laughter had a nervous ring that restored all my coolness and confidence.

"Our ten minutes are flying," I said; "it would be criminal to waste another second. Do you love me Madge?"

"No!" she cried, scarlet and astonished.

A whole minute went by before I spoke again.   Anyway I did not care for the remaining nine minutes,—now.

"Well," said I making an, effort to smile, "you knew that I loved you this morning,—there in the rose garden.   I had imagined that I could conceal it but —of course I was a self-confident idiot. You knew I loved you then, did you not?"

"No."

"Madge!   The ten minutes are not over yet."

She was silent.   I drew out my watch.

"Did you know it then?"

She turned her face away from me.

"Tell me," I urged, "these ten minutes will never come again, and we have all our lives to fib in.   Will you tell me?"

"Yes, I did!" she said suddenly.

"You knew that I loved you still?"

"Yes.   What time is it?"

"We have four minutes left, but there is nothing more to say.   I am going to deliberately stamp out my love for you, Madge, and it won't trouble either of us again. I began it this afternoon and," I went on pleasantly, " I will continue in the same lines. Don't be impatient,— you will make your lip bleed in another moment ;—I have only two more minutes to speak the truth in. I came here because I found the world intolerable—after you had gone. The day you came I believed myself cured. Now I know I am a very sick man. But I will be cured for both our sakes, Madge ; I 'll go back to the world and stir it up a bit. I 'll—"

" What time is it ?" she asked faintly.

" I have fifty seconds. That gives me just time to say that I love you. Three words,—and you don't know what they mean. I love you. And in ten seconds more I shall never say it again. In five seconds more I will begin to cure myself."

" What time is it," said Marjory.

" The last second has just ticked."

"Sten," she said quietly, " you might have offered me a minute or two out of those ten,—but they are gone—forever."

I looked at her in consternation.

"Too late," she said, "it's fibs now for the rest of our lives."

"Tell me one then!" I cried.

"I hate you," she laughed, and slipped away to join the Duchess.

"Is this game of battle-dore going on?" I thought angrily. "No! I'll stand no more torment; I'll trample out the last trace of tenderness in one way or another! I'll go to Caucasia and make plots and Kings! I'll kiss a pretty mouth too when I see it!"

Mops had lingered behind and Lina ran back to fetch him.

"Here he is," said I; "Lina, are you still superstitious about kissing?"

She said she was. The others were not in sight.

About half-past four that afternoon I strolled into the sunny grove on the borders of the Tschiska. The Duchess was seated upon a bank of moss, watching Lina, who had arrived, carrying Mops, a few minutes before I came.

Lina was now bathing Mops; her

sleeves were rolled up showing a pair of perfect white arms, her hair blew across her soft cheeks upon which two spots of carmine deepened and paled.

"There is some mistake here," thought I, looking from Lina to the Duchess and from the Duchess to Lina; "there is some awful mistake, that's certain. The Duchess should be washing the dog."

Now it was patent to anybody that Lina's small golden head was especially designed for a coronet, but what the head of the Dowager Duchess had been designed at all for, her Maker only knew. But the marvel of all lay in Lina's aristocratically perfect hands and feet.

I looked from the fat ankles of the Dowager Duchess von Schwiggle to the perfectly turned ankles of Lina.

"This," thought I, "is too serious for joking; fun is fun and von is von but I 'll eat Taxil's dace if Lina does n't deserve a *zu* in front of whatever comes after 'Lina.'" And I joined her Grace under the beech tree.

The King who had been earnestly conversing with Taxil beside the water's edge, now came up the bank and called us all around him.   And when we were seated at a sign from him, he turned to the Duchess with something of nobility in his gesture.

"My aunt," he said unaffectedly, "for the last time I will ask you not to force me to my throne again.   I am not fit; I know neither how to choose my ministers nor how to rob the people through them. The first I cannot learn, the last I refuse to learn.   Now, my aunt, am I fit for a King either way?"

"Yes," said the Duchess; "I will advise you."

"You have already attempted it," replied the King without bitterness.

"I was not in Belgarde.   I will go," boomed the Duchess.

The King turned instinctively to me.

"Will you be there?" he asked.

The gentle supplication in his eyes won me completely.

"I will," I answered firmly.

"As what?" demanded the Duchess, with an ominous ring in her deep voice.

" As whatever I choose," said the King haughtily.

"Give me a regiment," I cried,—"I ask for no pay; give me a regiment, your Majesty!"

Madge Grey leaned over to me, dropping her voice: "You never commanded soldiers!" she said; "I do not wish you to."

"'I'm going for a soldier now,'" I whispered laughing; "I'm going to stir up the world a bit. It owes me a little pleasure."

The King was looking at me all the time. I raised my head and smiled at him.

"I am not a military man," I said, "but with your Majesty's permission I'll try my hand at it. There will be fighting on the frontier before we enter. Let me recruit a regiment after my own fashion. I'll go bail your Majesty will hear from us."

"Do you want nothing in return?" asked the King incredulously.

"Nothing except exemption from any superior's orders."

General Bombwitz blew out his cheeks furiously and coughed three times.

"But," said the King, "I want you near me,—near to my person."

"That's just it," I replied calmly, "I propose to make my regiment your Body-guard, and to answer for your life and successful entry into Belgarde, with my own life and the lives of every trooper in my command."

The King's broad freckled face flushed.

"Life-guards do no fighting," he said.

"This Life-guard will lead in every fight! Your Majesty, hear me!—that is the only way a Monarch should re-enter his own,—with bared sword!"

"You are right!" said the King,—but in my other hand I shall bear free pardon for all."

"What!" cried the Duchess.

"For all!" repeated the King. "Mr. Steen, I accept your services."

"May I choose my officers?" I asked.

"Choose at will."

"Then I take his Grace of Taxil and his Grace of Babu," I said very loudly ;

"and I urgently solicit the aid and advice of General Bombwitz!"

A stupor seemed to seize the three mentioned gentlemen, but the King sprang to his feet and cried; "Obey!" And the three rose and came toward me, mechanically bringing their heels together and halting at attention.

"Gentlemen," I said, "his Majesty is going back to Belgarde or you and I won't linger very long in this pleasant world. I am going to recruit a regiment and you and I and that regiment are going to gallop behind his Majesty into Belgarde before the snow flies. Do your duty and you will be in at the death; shirk it and death will be into you. That is all."

Then I turned to the King and said; "Permit me, your Majesty, to suggest that you send General Bombwitz at once to the King of Caucasia."

"I will," said the King.

Bombwitz reddened with pleasure.

"He shall be off to-night," I said. "The two horses are good,—I will give him my milkman, Georgiades, as guide and escort."

"But," said the King," "suppose that in the meantime the Russian spies come into the valley?"

"Listen," I said, "I will see Constantine, my butcher. He lives in a little house on the Taxil high-road, just above the notch. If any stranger should pass through the notch he shall either come and warn us, or, if he has no time for that, he shall set a signal,—a red rag tied to a tree on the mountain side where anybody from the house can see it."

The King nodded and gave his hand to aid the Duchess who wanted to rise.

"One thing more," I said; "tell General Bombwitz to ask the King of Caucasia to send you £10,000 in gold. This Body-guard is going to be paid."

"You are learning military science very fast," said the King smiling; "it shall be done."

One by one we filed out of the grove and took the narrow path again. Lina's dainty figure was far in advance. She was obliged to bear Mops and the grunts of the Duchess.   I looked after her wistfully.

"Are you coming," said a low voice at my elbow.

"Yes," I said, "shall I lead, Madge?"

"No; walk beside me.   Why do you take this foolish risk?"

"What risk?"

"A soldier's?"

"Nonsense," I laughed—

"I 'll break the fighting line, as you broke your plighted vow,
For I 'm going for a soldier now!"

"Suppose—suppose I made another vow?"

But I swore under my breath that I had had enough of hell for this life and I did not reply.

"Sten," she said, "are you going?"

"Yes," I replied pleasantly.

Then we spoke of other things; how she, visiting the castle of Lauterschnapps on the Duchess' invitation, came to go first to the Austrian capital and then to the Tiflix Valley.

"It was very simple," she said; "my hostess the Duchess was obliged to go and I saw that it would be interesting, so I begged her to take me. When the Emperor of Austria was compelled to decline to receive the King, the Duchess set out to find him and warn him. In Sofia we learned he was on his way and we headed him off; that's all."

"When are you going back with the Duchess?" I enquired.

"Are you so anxious to see the last of me?" she asked abruptly.

"No. But you can't stay here and be mixed up in these plots and intrigues. If they catch us, you know, we will all follow Panitza and Stambouloff. Then what will you do?"

"I can take care of myself," she said, tossing her head.

By this time we had reached the high-road again.

"Sten," she said after a long silence, "don't do this thing."

"What thing?"

"Turn soldier."

I looked at her narrowly. "Would you have me back out?"

"Yes."

"But that is dishonorable. I am com-mitted."

"Oh!" said she bitterly, "what fools men are!"

"God begins us so," said I, "and wo-man finishes the work."

After a moment Madge said ; "Yes—but God made women also. It is not our fault."

So we two fools walked on along the dusty highway, comforting ourselves with the wisdom of our own folly.

CHAPTER VIII.

THE TOILET OF MOPS.

THE next day I sent Taxil to Paris. He bore a note from me to my old friend Clisson, ex-captain in the 50th Chasseurs d'Afrique. This was the note :

" Mon beau-sabreur :

" You are always grumbling because there is nothing going on. Now your chance has come. King Theobald of Boznovia wants six hundred young men who have cut their teeth and who know how to cleave other people's. If you want a commission to lead any such young men, it 's ready for you. The lighter their touch on hilt and trigger, the sooner they 'll touch their pensions. Their pensions and perquisites await them in Belgarde, but they must fetch them out on the points of their sabres.

If, by accident, six hundred such young men should meet in Bazoum, which city, you are aware, is the capital of Caucasia, it is dollars to doughnuts and francs to fromage that they would find six hundred horses awaiting them, six hundred scarlet tunics, and six hundred sabres. Draw on me at sight for what you need. Drexel is my banker.

In three weeks, then, in Bazoum.

"STEPHEN STEEN."

P.S. Is a field marshall's uniform becoming to you?"

I walked with Taxil as far as the notch in the mountains. Here Constantine, my butcher, was ready with an ein-spänner to drive him to the Ezrox Station on the Carpathian and Asiatic Railway.

"Good-bye," said I, pressing his hand, " you have plenty of money and plenty of time. I expect you to succeed."

Then I turned to the driver, my butcher : " Constantine, when you return from the station don't forget about your red signal rag if anybody enters the notch."

Constantine grinned and nodded.

Taxil drew me aside.

" You promise me a railroad from the Taxil Mines to Belgarde if I succeed?"

" Yes—the King has promised."

" But you?"

" The King has promised," I repeated.

Then I laid my hand lightly on his sleeve,—he wore an old coat of mine and looked like a well to do vine-grower.

"I forgot to tell you what I promise if you don't succeed," said I smiling.

"What?"

I pointed to a stone wall. "File of men and thirty seconds' grace."

We looked steadily into each other's eyes. I was satisfied. A moment later he went whirling away in the ein-spänner toward the Ezrox Station.

I walked thoughtfully back to the valley, switching the long grass with my mountain staff. Once or twice I thought of an illustration I had seen in *Harper's Weekly*,—Major Panitza shot to death in front of a dead wall.

When I reached the house the sky-larks were trilling and warbling in the sky, the thrushes sang in the thickets, the bullfinches whistled from the cherry trees. Gusts and dashes of music came from vineyards and maize fields, from garden, hedge, and pasture, until the whole blue atmosphere seemed saturated with song.

" There will be louder music soon," I thought, and I remembered bitterly how the dull boom of the cannon from the Genghis Pass had silenced every feathered chorister in the Tiflix Valley.

I found the King in his bed-room writing proclamations and manifestos.. I aided him for an hour,—he was a slow penman and a slower author,—and after a while he left it all to me and returned to the study of the map of Boznovia which I had found for him in my library.

Babu was in his room, — locked in and involuntarily undergoing a primitive Keeley cure on constantly reduced and diluted doses of cognac. The native Servian remedy, the powdered Ispha nut, he had refused to take at first, but, as the days passed and the rations of cognac grew smaller and weaker, he swallowed it in desperation, and recovered his appetite which the use of the nut invariably excites. So began the cure of his Grace of Babu.

The week wore away uneventfully It was too early yet to hear from General Bombwitz or from Taxil. Every morning I fixed my marine glasses on the notch, but no red signal rag fluttered from the designated tree top and I knew that so far we were safe. It had been agreed that the twenty-four hours should be cut into six watches, the Duchess, Madge Grey, Lina, Obadiah, the King, and myself, to take turns examining the notch with the field glasses. Babu, of course was exempt ; he was too earnestly occupied in getting cured to be trusted yet.

Constantine stretched a silk cord across the pass every night. One end of the cord connected with a bell just above his head. Occasionally a passing deer or chamois would ring him up and he would bound out of bed to investigate, ready, at sight of a human figure, to light and hoist his little red lamp on the pine tree above the notch. Once a great Carpathian bear snapped the cord and Constantine, rushing out, found the bear awaiting him in pleased surprise. It was a narrow escape and well worth the fifty marks that I gave him for his devotion.

Madge and I seldom saw each other

alone. She passed most of her time with the Duchess in their rooms. The King worked steadily at his maps and manifestos, and also on a list of proposed reforms for Boznovia, every one of which he discussed with me. Those that I recommended he retained, those that the Duchess approved he usually struck out.

I myself was studying German, French, English, and American cavalry tactics. The result was first chaos, then amended and revised tactics of my own. What knowledge I possessed of a military nature had been acquired while I was a trooper in the New York Dragoons, a volunteer battalion that was noted for its proficiency at banquets and cotillons. It's not such bad training either, for, although a little knowledge is dangerous, a great deal of knowledge sometimes prevents people from daring to do anything.

So I studied Upton, Esterhazy, Sheridan, and de Gallifet, until I did n't know the difference between horse-marines and horse-chestnuts ; and I gave it up.

"This regiment of mine," said I to myself, "shall be run by Steen's tactics, unadopted, unauthorized, and uncopyrighted. I 'll give the horses condensed fodder and cealine; I 'll give the men pemmican and Bull's concentrated beef pellets, and I 'll gallop them at anything that blocks the way to Belgarde. If the King of Caucasia does n't like it he can keep his opinion to himself; but I 'll bet that my troopers ride into Belgarde as soon as his."

One sunny afternoon toward the end of the week I left the King and his manifestos, and went down-stairs to the porch. It was Obadiah's watch. I saw him under the orchard trees, a battered brass telescope across his knees, staring toward the notch as though hypnotized.

"You 'd better close your mouth, 'Diah," I suggested, "you know some birds are nesting yet."

The cavern closed with a dazzling display of ivory.

"Whose watch is it next?" I asked.

"H'it am de Duchess watch, Mars' Steen," said Obadiah.

I looked at my time-piece.

"Go and notify her now. Has Miss Grey passed this way?"

"Yessah."

"Up the road?"

"Yessah."

I turned and looked up the white highway. Far away near the hill-top, a figure was silhouetted against the blue.

"Go and find her Grace," I said, and started up the road to overtake Madge Grey.

"She's going to make the tour by the Tschiska," I thought; "I'll surprise her in the woods by the mile post. Hello! She's taken that cursed lap-dog with her."

As I spoke the distant figure turned sharply into the woods just where the little forest path leaves the high-road by the mile post. I walked on at a good swinging pace, puffing my cigarette and glancing right and left across the clover-scented pastures where clouds of white butterflies drifted and eddied with every wandering breeze.

The bitter memory of what I had suffered from Marjory Grey's caprice had given place to a serene, almost contented acceptance of the situation.   A week ago she knew that I loved her, and I, knowing that she knew it, had asked·her if she loved me.   Her answer gave me a moment's agony, an hour's anger, and that ended it.

When her coquetry led her to allow me another ray of hope, I knew too much to be dazzled.   And now I had come to accept it as it was ; I had tried to stamp out the last ember of love for her, and I told myself that I had succeeded.   Angry pride and the philosopher's stone are said to be great transmuters.

When I came to the mile post I called aloud, and my voice echoed far in the forest, fainter, fainter, until the dry chatter of a magpie drowned the last lingering note.

"Now she 'll wait for me," I thought, and I entered the leafy path.

There were several reasons, I told myself, why I wished to join Madge Grey

on her afternoon walk ; one was because
I preferred any good company to my
own ; another, because the forest was not
perfectly safe.   Bears occasionally came
into the valley from their dens on the Osman Peak, and a she-bear with cubs was
downright dangerous.   The small wild-
cats never bothered people, although
again, a female with kittens had once
come at me sideways, spitting like mad,
back arched, and tail swollen half as large
as her body.   These I considered very
good reasons for joining Madge Grey.
To tell the truth, there was also a third
reason : I was not unwilling that Marjory should see how completely cured I
was.

So I strode on contentedly through
the trees, smelling the sweet wild wood
perfumes, stooping at times to pluck a
long stemmed orchid to add to the woodland bouquet for Madge's belt.

Once a thought came into my head
that bothered me.   It was this : Why, if
I was cured of my love for Marjory Grey,
should I quit my pheasants and trout and

rose-bowered house, to risk life, limb, and
fortune for a dull-witted Boznovian? Suppose it were possible to back out without
dishonor ; would I be satisfied now to
live the rest of my life in the Tiflix Valley?   At the very thought of it a horror
seized me.   No, it was impossible now.
Whatever it had been that stirred my
sluggish blood,—whether it was the coming of Madge, or the glimpse of the world
I had quitted,—whether it was the thirst
for action or merely the curiosity to see
how the King would bear himself, I did
not know.   One thing was certain ; the
valley was too small for me now.   Physical and mental activity I craved ; and I
stood a fair chance of being satisfied.

Thinking these thoughts I hastened on,
adding now and then to my bouquet of
white and orange orchids ; and at last I
caught the flutter of a gown ahead of me
and I saw a figure moving slowly through
the covert.

Suddenly Mops barked : the figure
turned.   It was not Marjory Grey.

I stood a moment silent, awkwardly

holding my bouquet of orchids.   Then I said :

"Lina, where is Miss Grey?"

"Miss Grey is ill with a headache, Mr. Steen."

"In the house?"

"Yes sir."

"It's that idiot Obadiah," I said smiling, "he mistook you for Miss Grey."

Lina looked at Mops.

"Lina," said I, "would Mops object if I walked a little way with you?"

"I don't know sir."

"Would you object?"

"Oh no sir,—if you wish to."

I walked up to her and slipped the orchids into her belt.   She said nothing. Mops growled.

"Shall we walk?" said I.

And we moved on.

She had taken off her hat and the sunlight filtering through the leafy roof above, burnished her small golden head.   She held the hat between the thumb and forefinger of her left hand and swung it gently as she walked.   A thrush peered at her from a Tucha-bush and sang three sweet notes; a cock-pheasant drummed the long roll in honor of her loveliness.

"Lina," said I, "this forest is very beautiful. It lacked a dryad before you came."

When I said this I was quite certain that Lina had never heard of dryads.

"Thank you," she said demurely, "I have often longed to live in a tree."

So she did know about dryads. I dimly wondered if it were possible that Lina was making fun of me.

"Would you rather I compared you to a water nymph?" I asked.

"It might be more suitable. I am going to wash Mops in the Tschiska."

I noticed that she had dropped the 'sir,' in speaking to me.

"Hm! I may be able to assist you," I said. "I observed last week that you leaned dangerously far over the pool. My arms are always at your disposal,— what are you singing, Lina?"

"I sing of arms and the man," she replied.

The silence lasted a minute.

"You are fond of Virgil?" I enquired coldly.

"In the original, Mr. Steen."

This was both astonishing and irritating. I knew that it was time to assert myself so I took her hand in mine, very gently, and slipped one arm around her waist. She said nothing. After a moment, I kissed her.

"Do you mind?" I asked.

"It is your duty to combat superstition," she said gravely.

"Then," said I enthusiastically, "I will begin again!"

"But I am already converted—"

"No, no!" I cried, horrified, "some doubts must still linger—"

"None."

"Not one?"

"Well—perhaps—one little one—"

Thus we passed through the forest, fighting our doubts and superstitions.

When we came to the Tschiska we sat down on the sunny bank, and she took Mops in her lap to remove his hideous pink ribbons.   He knew what that meant, and moaned.

"Yes," said I, appreciating his misery, "the water is cold! You may well moan and shiver, you nasty German lap-dog!"

"Poor Mops," remarked Lina.

"Poor Mops," I repeated hypocritically.

"You need n't say that," said Lina, "you know you hate him."

She carried him, struggling and yelping to the pool and rolled him in.   The miserable cur immediately swam out again.

"Let me fix him," I suggested.

"You won't hurt him?"

"I never hurt animals,—even perverted lap-dogs," said I, and I tossed Mops into the centre of the pool.

The dog swam at once, not back to the shore but out to a warm flat rock that lay half submerged in the middle of the Tschiska.

"Now," said Lina desperately, "he won't come back till we get up to go home."

It was true. Threats, entreaties, seductive whistling, had no effect. Mops sat on the warm rock and licked his dripping flanks, casting evil oblique glances at me.

"I am sorry," said I, possessing myself of one of Lina's small soft hands.

As we sat there, silent, listening to the ripple of the Tschiska among its pebbles, it came into my mind that the world was no whited sepulchre after all. I looked side-ways at Lina. How quiet she was, sweet and pale as a forest blossom. I remembered the Duchess von Schwiggle with her granitic face and her thick ankles.

"*Von* Schwiggle?" I thought to myself contemptuously; "her name should be Bauer and she should sell slabs of carp flesh in the Au on Fridays."

Lina raised her eyes to mine.

"What is your other name?" I asked gently.

"My other name, Mr. Steen?"

"Yes."

"I don't know that I shall tell you."

"Never mind," said I, "I know what it ought to be."

"What?—Mr. Steen."

"Oh *von* or *zu* something or other"—

"But—dear me!—I am not a German."

"Not German!"   I cried delighted, "there! I knew you could n't be!"

"But my name is Lina."

"That's true,—"

"Suppose I should tell you it is n't Lina?"

"Tell me then."

"But it is Lina."

"Oh."

"Not my first name."

"You have three names?"

"I have six.   I 've a mind to tell you some of them,—"

"Don't tease, Lina."

"Very well, my name is Dorothy—"

"Dorothea?"

"No, that's German; Dorothy Eileen Marguerite Inez—"

"You 're teasing again!"

"No, really, all those are my names."

"Then you are French.   Yet you don't speak French exactly as French people do—"

"Don't I," she laughed, clapping her small hands delighted.

" Oh tell me, Lina !"

" My last name ?"

" Yes,—please !"

" No," she said decidedly, " I will not tell you."

" It would be easy for me to ask the Duchess," I said laughing.

" The Duchess ! Oh, she 'll tell you that my name is Lina Cherbuez."

" And it is n't ?"

" No, it is n't."

" When did you enter the Duchess' service ?"

" The day she left schloss Lauter-schnapps." I was disappointed and she saw it.

" Listen," she said, " I went to her Grace well recommended and she took me because her own travelling companion was ill. I am not an ordinary maid, Mr. Steen."

" I know you 're a sweet little maid,—"

" I speak six languages," she said.

" Do you play ?"

" Harp, lute, violin, and piano,"

I looked down at her lovely aristocratic fingers.

"I was not mistaken," said I; "I might have known it also from your voice and language."

"What?"

"That you are well-born."

"I am not," she said slowly.

"Then who in Heaven's name is?" I cried.

"Her Grace the Dowager Duchess von Schwiggle," said Lina, and solemnly tossed a pebble into the water at our feet. Even the ripples laughed.

"Mr. Steen," she said as we rose to go; "I would rather you did not mention the list of my names and accomplishments to anybody until I give you permission."

Of course I promised, wondering a little.

"Come," she said, shyly holding out one hand.

We had gone perhaps a quarter of a mile when Mops appeared behind us.

"I knew he'd come," said Lina gaily.

"Who would n't?" I muttered.

The human heart is fearfully and wonderfully made;—so is the skeleton of the domestic mule.

CHAPTER IX.

THE SLUMBER OF THE DUCHESS.

WHEN we came in sight of the house I could see nobody but the Duchess. She was lying in a steamer chair under the trees, the brass telescope in her lap, her geological face turned toward the notch.

"Her Grace keeps good watch," said I ; "do you suppose she 'll raise Cain because you and I return together ?"

"I don't know," said Lina ; "I believe her Grace is asleep."

"Asleep !" I cried anxiously. We stood still, staring at the Duchess. I stepped forward, lifted the telescope from her Grace's lap, and levelled it at the notch.

The red rag was fluttering from the signal tree !

"Are you ill ?" asked Lina, "you have turned quite white." I handed her the glass and laid my hand on the Duchess' arm.

"Come," I said coldly, as she sat up gaping and blinking; "the signal flag is flying and who knows how long it's been there? Somebody is in the valley, how near nobody can tell. You have betrayed your trust, Madame; it's a bad beginning for an arch-conspirator."

"Herr Je!" gasped her Grace.

"Precisely," I replied, "he has us in his keeping. Go to the King, Madame, and bundle him out of sight. And keep yourself and Babu out of sight,—go quickly, Madame, or by Heaven I'll drop the whole affair!"

Lina assisted the dazed Duchess through the garden and into the house. I walked back to the porch, called Obadiah, gave him all necessary instructions, and sat down with my eyes fixed on the turn of the road.

I had not been there five minutes, when, without the least warning, two figures appeared, noiselessly speeding toward me, mounted on bicycles. Before I could rise they were at the gate, dismounted, and walking lightly up the path.

I returned their careful salute, and bade them enter.   There was no mistaking their faces ; they were Russians.

" Excelenz," said the taller man, who wore a rough English cycling suit, " I am looking for my master, the Duke of Taxil. Has he passed this way ? "

" A gentleman who called himself the Duke of Taxil passed through here," I replied.

" Alone ? "

" No," there were two others with him. They stopped at my house for a while."

" Were they hungry ? "

" Hungry and thirsty," I said laughing. " And if that is your condition also, pray come in."

" Thank you," said the taller man, speaking the beautiful English that many Russians master so easily, " we are rather pressed for time.   May I ask which way the Duke of Taxil and his party went ? "

" The Duke of Taxil passed through the notch at daybreak this morning."

The men exchanged glances. I could see that they were puzzled.

"Are you sure of this?" asked the taller man.

"Why yes. I saw him go."

"I only ask," continued the man, "because it was expected that he would go the other way toward Austria. Thank you, Excelenz,—no, we cannot stop,—we are much indebted to you."

"Now," thought I, "everything is easy. Let them chase Taxil to the notch. They never can guess that the old vine-grower who took the Carpathian and Asiatic Express is the Duke of Taxil. Besides they take it for granted that the King and Babu are with him. All is well," I thought gleefully, watching them where they stood preparing to mount their wheels. And all would have been well had not Lina suddenly appeared at the door. I heard her footstep behind me and turned, horrified. She looked at me, saw my frown, and at the same moment her eyes fell on the two cyclists. It took me only a second to make up my mind.

"Of course, my dear," I said, rising and taking Lina's hand affectionately, "I will ask them to wait long enough to drink a stirrup cup." And I walked out to the gate smiling.

"My wife," said I, "thinks that I show small hospitality and begs you will wait until she can send you a stirrup cup to speed you on your journey."

The two cyclists bowed. I could detect nothing in their faces which might not have been natural under the circumstances. At a signal from me, Obadiah brought out a bottle of Burgundy and three glasses. We all turned and bowed gravely to Lina, who replied with a quiet inclination of her pretty head ; then we touched glasses and solemnly emptied them.

A moment later the cyclists were wheeling away full speed toward the notch and I walked back to the porch, biting my moustache.

"By jingo !" I said, "that was a close call, Lina. Whatever in the world brought you down. Suppose they had known I was n't married ?"

"It was an accident," she said, "will Mr. Steen permit me to felicitate him on his perfect sang froid?"

In her eyes and voice there was the faintest tinge of irony, and I resented it.

"It was the best I could think of," I said sulkily; "luck was with me I admit. Why did you come down?"

"I heard no sound and how was I to know they had come? Mops is in the garden and I thought I ought to dry him. The Duchess would be inconsolable if Mops caught cold—"

"Mops! Mops!" I stammered furiously,—"between Mops and her Grace we'll all be ruined!" Lina turned away and I walked angrily across the garden to the orchard.

"I gave Lina credit for more sense than she has," I muttered, throwing myself into the steamer chair and fixing the marine-glasses on the signal tree. Ten minutes later I lowered the glasses with a long drawn sigh.

The signal flag was gone.

That evening at dinner we discussed

it very seriously. The Duchess, over-whelmed with rage and mortification, made no sound except when she sucked her soup from the spoon. Madge Grey, the King, and I agreed that the men were spies and Russians. The King had peeped at them through the curtains and he insisted that they were Russians from the Caucasus.

"I know the breed," he said, "you can't mistake those eyes and cheek bones. Well, I'm glad it's all right but it was a narrow margin for some of us."

I looked at Lina. She stood at the Duchess' elbow, demure, pensive as a tired kitten.

"Where the devil," thought I, "did she get her beautiful hands?"

Dinner over, the Duchess, Madge, and Lina, withdrew to their rooms; the King retired to smoke his faience pipe and com-pose "An Appeal to the Powers"; and Babu and I wandered aimlessly from the deserted drawing-room to the smoking-room, then through the dim library and the gun-room, out onto the porch.

"I trust your Grace is improving," said I, "the Ispha nut is an astonishing remedy."

"Yes," said the Duke with a grimace, "it is more astonishing than the disease."

"But," I insisted, "you are better; anybody can see that. You have an appetite that is simply royal."

"That's just it," muttered Babu, "it's too much for a Duke. You are diluting my cognac with water—"

"Of course: to-morrow I'm going to dilute your water with cognac. It's the only way: I'll have no drunkards in my regiment and I have you slated for Captain."

"That's all very well," said his Grace sulkily, "but I'm a naval officer, or rather I was, and I don't care for cavalry service."

I thought of the single gun-boat of the Boznovian navy and looked at the Admiral.

"Do you miss the sea?" I asked gently.

"Well no," replied the Duke, "I was always on shore duty because my flag-ship ran on a sand bar and the King let it stay there."   Then he leaned close to me and whispered confidentially ; " The truth is the Boznovian navy was a farce."

" No ! " I exclaimed.

" It was," he insisted, wagging his head and shutting his great round eyes.

After a moment he drew out a bon-bon-nière, swallowed a morsel of Ispha nut with every symptom of displeasure, and said good-night.   I looked after him, nodding to myself contentedly, then I lighted my cigarette and sank into a big cane arm-chair in a corner of the porch.

The long summer day was nearly ended. Pale streaks of light still lingered in the west, fading slowly from faintest rose to pallid yellow.   High in the evening air swallows still twittered and house-martins wheeled and squealed, soaring in circles above weather-vane and chimney-pot. From the lower branches of the apple-trees came the plaintive peep of roosting chickens and the querulous notes of sleepy turkeys ; and I heard the drowsy quack-ing of ducks and the murmur of geese among the sedges of the meadow mere.

10

A star broke out in the darkening zenith, then another and another, and still others, and now they were everywhere, glimmering, sparkling, clustering from horizon to horizon.   Had the night fallen so swiftly? I looked around.   The great hawk-moths were hovering among the lilies, now only pale patches in the garden's dusk.   Far in the forest an owl hooted twice.   Mist shrouded the pond.   It was night.

And with the night came Madge Grey, softly stepping among the roses, pushing aside the perfumed branches that hung heavily across the path.   She did not see me at first,—it was the glow of my cigarette tip in the dusk that warned her.

I found a big chair for her, and when she was comfortable, I resumed my seat in the corner.   For a long time we sat there in silence ; I let my cigarette go out and dropped the end on the lawn.

She spoke first,—saying something about home, I believe.   I heard her, but I scarcely comprehended what she said. I was thinking, marvelling that the sound of her voice no longer set my heart beating,—no longer sent that long thrill to the tips of my limbs. Did I love her yet? Upon my soul I could not have answered that question.

Presently I heard myself asking : "Are you sometimes a little homesick, Madge ?"

"Yes, sometimes."

"Now ?"

"Yes.   Perhaps it is the perfume of the lilies—"

"When is the Duchess going ?"

"As soon as the Duke of Taxil returns with the horses."

"Ah !" I exclaimed, "true—she can't go without the horses.   I am hoping that Taxil may return to-morrow."

"So soon ?"

"It's nearly a week,"

"It has passed swiftly for me," she said simply.

I was on my guard at once.   That low voice would never play the devil with me again !

"Then the Duchess, I suppose, will take you back to schloss Lauterschnapps with her ?" I asked pleasantly.

"Oh yes, I suppose so. I dread it, Sten."

"Why? Is n't the schloss cheerful? Tell me a little about this stony faced Dowager and her stony ribbed castle."

"If you like; it's not gay,—you may light a cigarette if you wish, Sten ;—no, it is not very gay, the castle of Lauterschnapps.   I went there because you know the Duchess is very fond of Mamma.. She stood up for her when Papa ran away with her.   Imagine, Sten, how it must feel to have a mother only a year or two older than yourself,—and oh so beautiful ! They say that Mamma is one of the most beautiful women who ever came to Berlin, and by far the loveliest that ever entered castle Lauterschnapps,—except the Princess Sylvia—"

"Who ?"

"The Princess Sylvia,—you know,— the one they call ' Witch Sylvia.'"

"But I don't know," I insisted ; "is she a German Princess ?"

"Why no.   I mean the Princess Sylvia of Marmora.   Her brother was put on

the Boznovian throne, a few days ago, by
the Czar. You must have heard of him ?"

"I believe I have," said I, smiling ;
"is n't she the one who scandalizes all
Europe by doing what she pleases ?"

"Of course. And when she was younger
she was a great favorite with the Duchess
von Schwiggle, but it has been four years
since the Duchess has seen her. Do
you know what Witch Sylvia did ? She
appeared one morning at a schloss boar-
meet, dressed like a page of the sixteenth
century ! Imagine the horror of the
Duchess. She has never set eyes on the
Princess Sylvia since."

"I should like to have seen it all the
same," said I.

"Oh, they say she was simply exquisite,
with her blue eyes and silky dark curls,
and her hose and doublet and hawks-
feather.—Really I don't see so very much
harm in that, do you ?"

"I ? Not at all."

"Neither do I. But I am afraid that,
since then, her escapades have not been
exactly proper. She went for a whole

week to the Carpathian army manœuvres dressed like a Moldovian Hussar, and nobody found it out until the Moldovian attaché complained. They say when Bismarck heard of it he laughed more than he had since England was chased out of the Transvaal."

"But," said I, "what did her brother do?"

"Her brother? He's afraid of her."

"He must make a fine King for Boznovia," I observed.

"No worse than Theobald of Taximbourg," said Madge, dropping her voice. "It is simply a crazy scheme to try to force him back on the Boznovian people."

"It will be easy," said I, "if this Prince of Marmora is the sort of man who is afraid of his sister."

"True," she said, "but if his sister, the Princess Sylvia, undertakes to repel your invasion, I would n't give three bronze pfennings for the chances of Theobald of Boznovia."

"We will see," said I, somewhat nettled.

" Ah, that is just what I am afraid of. Don't—don't go on this expedition. You know what the end will be if you. fail—"

I thought again of the picture in *Harper's Weekly*.

" Listen, Sten, give it up and dissuade the King. You are no soldier,—you were not bred to it—"

" I was . in the New York Dragoons—"

" But you don't understand—you don't know what these European armies are."

" Yes I do."

" And you don't realize what this Witch Sylvia is capable of—"

" Was she trained for a soldier? I think that I may venture to match my wits against hers, Madge."

" But Witch Sylvia is consulted even by the Chief of the general staff."

" Bother Witch Sylvia !" I muttered.

CHAPTER X.

THE WAY OF A MAID.

THE next day passed without any news from Caucasia. I was growing restless.. Hour after hour I started up, imagining that I heard the sound of hoofs on the high-way, but when I hurried to the porch there was nothing moving on the white road, stretching to the hill on the northern horizon. Babu, greatly depressed by a heroic dose of Ispha nut, mooned about the garden, smoking strong cigars until I wished he would go away. The Duchess had a headache and Madge Grey was watching the notch. The King still labored over his " Appeal to the Powers "; I could hear him breathing hard behind his closed door. The scratching of his pen irritated me.

About one o'clock his Grace of Babu

went fishing in the Tschiska.   I was glad
to get rid of his depressed countenance
and I cheerfully lent him a good rod and
directed him to the best water.   Obadiah
went with him as instructor and gilly,
promising to return in time to get dinner.

When they had gone I began to wan-
der about the house, probably wearing a
more dismal face than poor Babu's, and
at last I went into the kitchen to see how
Obadiah had left affairs.   The first thing
I noticed was Mops, sniffing at a plate of
preserves on the table.   The next thing I
saw was Lina, writing in a little book.

She did not hear me,—I wore noiseless
espadrilles,—and I came close to her and
touched her lightly.

She turned like a flash.

"Why, Lina!" I laughed, "I did n't
mean to startle you so.   Forgive me,—
really I had no idea of frightening you."

As I spoke the color slowly returned to
her face and she smiled also.

"It was very indelicate of you," she
said ; "I might have been writing a love
letter."

" But you were not."

" No, only a receipt for kilash. Are you fond of kilash ? "

" Rather. I don't think much of Servian dishes."

" Then I must make you some of my kilash. Oh' you will like it. Don't you think you had better release my hand ? "

" It is a beautiful hand ! " I said. My own earnestness amazed me.

" It is pretty—for a maid."

" For an Empress," I added gravely.

" And—my figure ? " she asked with a daring smile.

" It is marvellous," I said truthfully ; " your head is perfect too, your ears, your delicious nose, your mouth, your eyes, your—"

" Dear me ! You approve then ? "

" I ? Why Lina you are the most exquisite creature I have ever seen ! "

I doubt if Lina was more astonished than I was at this outburst. It was the truth and it had suddenly flashed upon me that she was the rarest thing on earth, a perfectly beautiful woman. Still I was scarcely prepared to tell her so. It said itself involuntarily,—my lips were but mechanical agents, my tongue wagged of its own accord.

" Mr. Steen," she said at last, " do you think that is the way to speak to a lady's maid ? "

" It is the truth," I muttered.

" But a gentleman,—a well-born man cannot think seriously of a—a—"

" What ? A lady's maid ? "

" Yes."

" That," said I sincerely, " would have no weight with me, if I loved."

" A servant ? You ? "

" If you were that servant,—and I loved you," I repeated.

" But you don't,—you can't—"

" I don't know whether I do or not," I said frankly. " When I was not serious I thought lightly of kissing you, but now, upon my soul I am thinking it is more serious than charging a battery."

" And you dare not,—again ?

" Kiss you ? "

" Yes."

There was a reckless light in her blue eyes, a dash of carmine on either cheek.

"I dare," I said.

"Against my will?"

Before she knew what I was about I had kissed her once, full on the lips. It was the first time I had kissed her lips.

The color flamed in her cheeks; I was not very calm myself. Unconsciously we stepped back and looked at each other.

"Was it against your will?" I asked. My breath came rather fast and I attempted to smile easily.

"You did not ask me," she said slowly.

Then a strange terrible light flashed in her eyes, and in a second she had struck me. Dazed, doubting my senses, I stepped back, raising my hand to my stinging cheek.

I don't know how long we stood there, staring into each other's eyes, but after awhile I saw her eyes begin to dim a little, then droop to the floor.

"Pardon," she whispered.

I looked at her curiously. "I am the one to ask pardon," I said; "I have my deserts."

She leaned back, resting her hand on the table.

"Any man," said I coldly, "who lays himself open to a rebuke from an—an—"

"—Inferior!" she faltered.

"Gets his just dues," I ended.

A bright tear-drop fell from between her fingers.   Her head sank lower.

"And," said I, "any man who is ashamed to do what I do,"—here I took her right hand gently,—"and who would not ask pardon, as I do—" here I bent on one knee, —"and any man who would not dare to say, I love you—as I now say it, is no man, be he king or peasant!   I love you, Lina.   Will you marry me?"

Her left hand fell from her wet eyes.

"Yes," she said in a low earnest voice, "I will marry you—if I ever marry, for I love you."

She came up to me and deliberately kissed me.

"Our last, until we marry," she said; "you will respect my wish.   I must go to the Duchess; are my eyes red?   There, —yes—but only my hand.   I will be in the lower garden to-night after the Duchess retires.   I wish to see you,—I love you, do you understand?   Ah do you know what love is to me—to me?"

I trembled as I looked into her glorious eyes.   Her parted lips burned crimson.

"No," she said, shaking her head, "no you don't know yet what love is to me. You will know some day.   Take my hand. Do you feel how the palm burns?"

She withdrew her hand and slipped by me like a shadow, and was gone.   I turned uncertainly toward the door.   As I passed, Mops growled.   My cheek was still tingling from the blow, my heart was on fire.   Love is strange.   I know of but one definition for Love and that is, *Love*. Some call it insanity.   The synonym is inadequate.

CHAPTER XI.

WHEN Lina left me to find the Duchess, she left a very much bewildered young man. To marshall my disordered thoughts and inspect them as a drill-sergeant inspects his awkward squad, was my intention. I tried hard; it was useless.

Now whenever I am troubled and perplexed I go fishing. It is the best way to bring disorderly thoughts under discipline. So I picked up a rod and fly-book, slung a gun over my shoulder in case a thieving fox should court destruction, and walked out into the garden.

It was Madge's watch and I glanced up at her window to see if she was on duty. The end of the battered brass telescope projected a few inches beyond the sill.

"Are you there, Madge ?" I called.

"Yes."   She leaned from the window and looked down at me.   "Everything is quiet in the notch," she said, "are you going to fish the Tschiska ?"

"Yes, I 'll be back soon.   It 's time for the King's watch.   Will you notify him ?"

She nodded brightly and I lifted my cap and turned away into the high-road.

" I no longer love Madge Grey," said I to myself ; "that is certain, for I am not ashamed of what I 've done.   Madge is a sweet lovely girl,—I do like her immensely,—I almost love her—"

Here I lighted a match on the sole of my shoe and applied it to my pipe.

" I am cured—" puff ! puff !—" or I don't know what a—" puff—"a cure is.   I can't help it if she resents it ; she did—" puff ! "did it herself.   A fellow's love can't flourish on snubs."

Thus I walked on, avoiding the really vital question,—my sudden passion for Lina, and my impetuous, almost involuntary declaration.   I say I avoided it, and I did until I entered the forest by the mile post ; but here, in this sweet scented path where yesterday I had walked with Lina and—O delicious memory ! I had kissed her,—here the issue was not to be avoided. I faced it squarely and at the first retrospective glance, I saw that I was fully committed,—that I was compelled by every law of honour to stick by my words of this afternoon. At the thought that I was irrevocably bound to make good my protestations, a delightful exhilaration took possession of me.

"She is the loveliest in all the world !" I cried aloud again and again. The grey rocks echoed my words, "in all the world —all the world !—the world !" and the dim forest trees murmured assent.

A great happiness,—not turbulent, not linked with restlessness or trepidation, stole over me,—a happiness, peaceful, satisfying, serene.

"Then this is love," I thought. "It's not like the other."

White orchids with orange crowns nodded to me from the undergrowth as I passed. I remembered the bouquet I had slipped into her belt,—the same bouquet that I had expected to offer to Marjory Grey. It troubled me little as to what Marjory would say when the time came to tell her. What the Duchess or the rest of the world might think I did n't even trouble myself to consider.

"If Marjory cares for my friendship she must accept Lina without reserve," I thought. "If she will not, I shall lose a friend and regret it, but I 'd lose my trust in Heaven before I 'd budge from the woman I love !"

I was near the Tschiska now ; I heard the ripple and rush of water above the sighing forest leaves. In a dozen strides I came in sight of the river bank and at the same moment I stopped short in my tracks.

A great Carpathian bear was seated on its haunches in the middle of the path.

The brute had not heard me, for I still wore the soft espadrilles. I cautiously stepped back, unslung my fowling-piece, and sniffed for the wind. The wind was right—blowing from the bear to me.

"Confound the bear!" said I to myself, fingering my light fowling-piece ruefully, "it would be sheer madness to fire this pop-gun at a brute like that!"

The breeze being south the bear had not winded me. If it was only a he-bear I should n't have cared, for the brute would have made off at the first sniff of tainted air. Was this a he-bear? I was about to take the chances and shout,— first selecting a friendly tree of the proper shape in case of an emergency,—I say that I was on the point of shouting, when, from the river bank ahead, came the sound of a human voice,—a muffled yell, despairing, terrified, sad past all belief. I knew that voice. It was the voice of Obadiah.

Again the wail was repeated, and another voice, unmistakably belonging to his Grace of Babu, answered. The bear raised its head. Then it flashed upon me what the true state of the case was. Very gently I parted the branches, holding my breath, and looked out. I was right; the bear was a she-bear, for there, rolling about on the moss below the river bank, were two cubs; and above, directly in line with the old bear's nose, perched high among the limbs of a great spruce tree, squatted his Grace of Babu.

I could not see Obadiah at first, but after a while I espied him in the branches of an oak; and as I caught sight of him he wailed again, dismally.

"G'wuf'f'm hyah!" urged Obadiah, rolling his eyes at the bear; "ef Mars' Steen come hyah he cotch yo' sho' an' he bus' yo' cubs in de haid!"

Babu said nothing but he looked exceedingly unhappy.

"Mine yo' own business," urged Obadiah, scowling at the bear; "mine yo' own business an' g'wuf'f'm hyah. Ef yo' doan' git, 'Diah gwine hoodoo yo' cubs wif de rabbit-foot! Yas, ole 'Diah he gwine work de rabbit-foot,—" here Obadiah pretended to feel in his pocket for the alleged witch-charm.

"If you don't keep quiet," said Babu sulkily, "the bear won't go, will he?"

"Yessah!" said Obadiah. He did n't understand Babu who spoke only French and German beside his native tongue. "Yessah," said Obadiah, "I 'se gwine work de rabbit-foot sho' ef dat ole idgit doan' mosey.   I 'se gwine spile her cubs,—I 'se gwine—"

"Imbecile!" muttered Babu, "keep quiet, can't you!"

"Yessah," replied Obadiah cheerfully. "Das what I 'se gwine do, sah.   Dat ole she-bear fink 'Diah aint got no rabbit-foot—"

The bear rose and shambled to the foot of Obadiah's tree.   Babu looked on with interest.   Slowly the shaggy mustard coloured brute stood up, pushed her muzzle along the tree trunk, sniffed and wrinkled her nose, and then to my horror, deliberately began to ascend the tree. Obadiah fled howling to the top-most branches.

There was only one thing to do ; the bear was already in the second crotch and was mounting swiftly.   In an instant I had slung my gun across my back, leaped out, jumped down the river bank, and seized one of the small cubs in my arms.

Then I shouted with all my lungs. Slowly the bear turned, saw me, saw the cub wriggling and clawing in my arms. She gave a roar which was half growl, half shrill snuffle, and came tumbling down the tree, making the twigs and bark fly. I flung the cub into the river ; it fell with a mighty splash and began sprawling and thrashing toward the bank. Then I motioned Babu and Obadiah to get ready to run as soon as the bear started after me, and I waded into the Tschiska and floundered across.

As I gained the opposite bank I heard the bear plunge into the pool ; but whether she stopped to rescue her cub or whether she started on after me, I never knew, for I ran up the wood-road and took the first *sentier* to windward, and in a quarter of an hour I emerged, panting, dishevelled and soaked with perspiration, upon the high-road. Almost at the same instant, Obadiah, livid with terror, burst out of the wood a little farther down, followed closely by the Duke of Babu. His Grace was in a state of collapse when I arrived, and I advised him to lie down a bit in the grass.

"As for you, you leather headed jack-ass," I said to Obadiah, "it's a wonder you were not eaten by the she-bear for yelling like an Indian and telling a lot of lies about your rabbit's-foot. The children in the Bible were swallowed and digested for less."

"Mars' Steen," gasped Obadiah, "you fink dat ole she-bear knowed dat I di 'n hab no rabbit-foot?"

"Of course," said I severely, "and I tell you the bad little boys who cried 'go up bald head!' were innocent alongside of a bad darkey who tells lies and steals strawberries and melons."

This impressed Obadiah so profoundly that I was obliged to cheer him up a little. He tearfully acknowledged his sins, blubbered, moaned, but finally at my command went to a little rivulet which trickled down the rocks beside the road, and brought my pocket-cup full of water for the Duke of Babu.

When his Grace had sufficiently revived to start toward home, I began to question him about the bear. What he told me startled me more than the bear had. It seemed that while he and Obadiah were fishing in the Tschiska, they heard a call for help. Hurrying in the direction of the sound they had come upon very much the sort of scene that I witnessed,—the bear sitting under a tree, and a man clinging to the branches above. As soon as the man saw them he cried out to them in Russian, and at the same time the bear winded them and started in their direction. They had time to get to the Tschiska but not to cross it. Obadiah unhesitatingly swarmed up a tree and Babu followed his example, just too late for the bear to nip his heels.

"What became of this—this Russian?" I asked, as the Duke of Babu finished and wiped his face.

"I suppose he ran," replied his Grace.

"Do you understand Russian?" I persisted.

"Only a few words. The man cried;

'Help! in the name of the Holy Virgin!' I understood that."

" Don't you know which way he went ?"

"No," said Babu indignantly, "I didn't wait to ask him. This is a delightful country to fish in, but I think I can manage to live without any Tiflix valley fish after this. I lost the rod, the creel, my pipe, and all my Ispha nut."

" I 'll get you all the Ispha nut you want," said I, "but this Russian bothers me more than I can tell you. He couldn't have come through the notch for there was no signal and Constantine is trustworthy. If he didn't come that way he must have come from Caucasia; and now I am wondering what the devil a Russian spy was doing in Caucasia. If Russia finds out that we are mobilizing in Bazoum, the game is up."

" Perhaps he 'll be eaten by bears," suggested Babu hopefully.

" We 'll all be swallowed by a bigger bear than that," said I, "if Russia trees us in the Triflix valley. What is that you hold in your hand ?"

"Something I picked up in the path before that cursed bear treed me. Do you know what it is?"

"Why yes," said I, "it belongs to Lina, —to the Duchess' maid. It is that little gold Sainte-Catharine that she wears pinned at her throat."

"Oh," said Babu, "I found it on the other side of the Tschiska; I did n't know that the maid had been there."

"The other side!" I asked astonished.

"Yes. I thought the Russian might have dropped it. They are common pins."

"Perhaps he did then," I said. "It looks to me like that pin that Lina wears."

"Ask her," suggested Babu.

We were in sight of the house now.

"Give me the pin," said I, "and I will return it to her if it is hers." The Duke handed me the pin in silence. In a moment more we were passing through the garden to the porch where the King sat, his eye glued to the end of the telescope.

"I wish," said the King, "that you would look over my 'Appeal to the

Powers.'   There is something wrong about it and I can't just determine what. Ought I to say anything about Corea?"

"No indeed!" I said with emphasis, "let Corea alone.   What has Boznovia to do with the Chinese Question?   Steer clear of Turkey and China, your Majesty, and avoid any mention of India, Egypt, Hawaii, Samoa, and Cuba.   It is the Duchess' watch I believe.   Shall I notify her Grace?"

"I will tell her," replied the King, lowering the telescope and handing it to Babu.   "Come and see what I have written, Mr. Steen."

All that afternoon I worked on the 'Appeal to the Powers' while the King slept on the bed beside me.   At times I would rise to see whether the Duchess was again slumbering at her post.   There she sat in the garden below, waving a palm-leaf fan to keep the gnats away, raising the telescope occasionally with the automatic regularity of a mechanical doll.

The long day was coming to an end before I shoved the papers and ink bottle away from me and rubbed my tired eyes. A moment later Obadiah announced dinner and I awoke the King and went out into the garden to relieve the Duchess.

"If your Grace will kindly send Obadiah to me with a bottle of Rhenish and a sandwich I will watch while the rest dine," I said.

The Duchess fanned herself and examined me with hard eyes.

"Our vigilence must be redoubled, Madame," said I; "there is a strange man in the Tiflix valley. Heaven knows where he came from, unless from Bazoum!—and I wish to know whether he leaves the notch to-night, or whether we must stay indoors all day to-morrow. His Grace of Babu will tell the company at dinner what we have seen to-day."

The Duchess was silent, but her eyes were fixed on the lapel of my jacket where I had pinned the little gold Sainte-Catharine.

"This is part of the story," said I, touching it with one finger.

"Where did you get it?" asked the Duchess in her deep, ominous voice.

I told her.

"Do you recognize it?" I asked.

Yes," snapped the Duchess.

"Then it is your maid's," I said, unfastening it and handing it to her.

"It is not my maid's," replied the Duchess.   There was a note of something that resembled alarm in her voice.

"If you know this jewelled pin," said I, "will you not tell me where you have seen it?   I think anybody will recognize the necessity of clearing up this affair."

The Duchess took the pin from my out-stretched hand and examined it earnestly.   There was no mistake ; her Grace was certainly more or less affected.

" This pin," said the Duchess, at length, "is hollow, and it contains a lock of hair from the head of Sainte-Catharine of Russia."

I looked at her in amazement.

" I ought to know," she said angrily, " I had the pin made for a minx who pretended to be a respectable member of society.   I gave it to her.   I have never seen her since."

"Witch Sylvia !" I cried excitedly, and sprang from my chair. The Duchess also rose, her stern face working convulsively.

"How dare you name her in my presence !" she demanded ; "how dare you !"

"Madame !" I said, "this is no time for petty jealousy or private enmity. If Witch Sylvia has passed through this valley its for one reason, to find out what the King is doing. And if she has been here,—dare-devil that they say she is, it may be possible,—it was from Caucasia,—from Bazoum that she came !"

"It is impossible ! " stammered the Duchess, "she can't have so far forgotten herself as to come—spying here—like a common soldier !"

"Then where did that pin come from ? " I asked sternly. "Remember what Witch Sylvia did at the Carpathian manœuvres ! If she 's capable of putting on a hussar's trousers once, she 'll wear trousers again when she chooses. And Madame, I solemnly believe that if the Princess Sylvia should take it into her head to come into Tiflix valley, she would do it !"

The Duchess seemed dazed. She handed me the pin, shuddering as though the mere contact affected her.

"Look again, Madame, do you positively recognize this pin ?"

"Look yourself," cried the Duchess furiously, and stalked into the house, trembling with rage and fear.

"The old griffin !" I muttered, turning the pin over and over in my hand,—" ha ! by jingo ! she 's right, for here 's the inscription ; 'To Sylvia, from her affectionate Hedwig von Schwiggle !'" ·

"Affectionate !" I sneered, — " that lump of stony malevolence ? How the mischief did the pin come here in the forest ? The Princess Sylvia could n't have been here,—that 's all nonsense. Ten to one she lost it and somebody found it,—possibly the latest owner,—the Russian who was treed by the she-bear."

Night came as I sat uneasily pondering. I had changed the telescope for my marine glass which could also be made into a field glass or a night binocular by the mere turning of the rubber button. Two red lanterns would be the signal if the strange man attempted to leave the valley by the notch ; one, if any new-comer entered.

I was beginning to feel hungry and I cast impatient glances toward the dining-room. It would not have surprised me if the Duchess had forgotten or deliberately neglected to send me my Rhenish and sandwich. One by one, through the lighted windows, I saw the company rise and leave the table ; the King first, deep in conversation with Babu, the Duchess soon afterward, leaning on Madge Grey's arm. Then I saw Lina, giving some directions to Obadiah, who presently disappeared, carrying a pile of plates.

I waited in silence, expecting to see him come out with my dinner. At last, disgusted and hungry, I was on the point of calling out to him, when the door opened and Lina appeared bringing a covered tray.

" I have kept you waiting," she said in

a low mocking voice, " but I told you that I should make you some kilash from my own receipt and I thought that I might not have another chance—very soon. Are you angry,—and hungry ? "

" Hungry," I said, dropping my voice, " but only to see you again. Have they gone ? Can you stay ? "

" The Duchess is furious about something or other. She has retired to her room with Miss Grey. She insists upon leaving the valley to-morrow, horses or no horses."

" She may insist," said I, " as much as she pleases, but of course she can't do it. The Ezrox station is twenty miles beyond the notch. Ah Lina, we shall not be parted just yet,—you and I—"

A step on the porch interrupted me.

" Mr. Steen," said the King, " my aunt the Duchess insists upon leaving to-morrow. Will it not be dangerous for her to travel publicly before we are ready to join the Caucasian army in Bazoum ? "

" Certainly your Majesty," I said.

" It makes me very nervous," sighed

the King, " I wish to Heaven that my aunt would mind her own business ! "

" Be comforted," said I, " her Grace cannot leave the valley until the horses return. Has your Majesty decided on any course of action in regard to the man in the forest ? "

" I," said the King ; " no, I 'm worn out with trouble and worry. I can't see that the Duke of Babu has any more brains when he 's sober than when he 's not. He has gone to bed now ; he says the Ispha nut makes him so hungry that if he did n't sleep he 'd be eating every half hour. The Duchess won't speak to me ; she 's locked her door. Miss Grey is with her. I think I had better retire too. Have you had your dinner ? "

I pointed to the tray which Lina had set on a table beside me.

" Kilash ? " said his Majesty sniffing the air. " I love kilash,—but I suppose I 'll be living on beef pellets before long. Good night Mr. Steen,—send the maid up—when you are ready."

" Good night your Majesty," I said.

The King turned and, acknowledging Lina's profound curtsey, passed into the house.   He wore the saddest face I have ever seen.

"Poor tired unhappy little bourgeois," I thought, "God send you a sunny window seat, and all the kilash you can eat."

Then I turned to Lina and would have taken her in my arms but she slipped back with a pretty gesture and touched one finger to the covered tray.

"Your kilash is waiting, Monsieur," she said, "is my labor in vain? See, I burnt the tip of my finger making for you your kilash. No—no—you must not! hush! they may hear you."

"Then come out under the trees," I said, lifting the tray and stepping into the garden.

"For two minutes then—only two minutes," she whispered.

I set the tray down on the soft turf under the trees in the pasture.

"Will you sit beside me?" I asked. "Here is my jacket,—you will not feel the dew." She settled herself daintily on the grass and looked demurely at the tips of her shoes.

"Are you not going to begin?" she asked. "Really if I had imagined that you cared so little for my kilash—"

"Nonsense!" I said, whisking off the cover and picking up a fork,—"by jove! it is delicious! I'll take back whatever I have said about Servian dishes. This is ambrosia! Does the burnt finger hurt, Lina! You little angel, if you knew how I loved you—"

"Of course," she said calmly, "a man's heart resides in his stomach."

I looked at her half angry, half laughing.

"It does," she repeated; "all men are the same,—all men seek only the gratification of their own pleasure, be that pleasure power, or money or knowledge or appetite—Ah! wait until I have finished, you silly man,—I was going to say, "all men are alike except—you! Now are you contented?"

She suddenly leaned forward on the grass and looked into my face. Through the luminous starlight her eyes glittered almost fiercely.

"Are you contented!" she said again; "I love you—I love you. Don't you know it? Can you not see it in every movement, every breath that I draw? Ah men! men! how I have hated them and despised them!" she murmured through her little white teeth; "how well I have read them and understood them!" Then with another swift change: "Read me, read me if you can, O man whom I love! You cannot,—see!—you cannot. You are perplexed, you don't know what to make of me. But I know you. Are you contented?"

She sat up, breathless, smiling again. As for me, she had carried me away with her. My ears were echoing with the fierce passion in her voice; I was completely dazed.

"You did n't know what a little cyclone you started when you—you kissed me that first day in the garden," she said. "Suppose I should tell you that I, a poor serving-maid, had never before been kissed. Would you believe me?—hush! —I know you do. It is true. Never before has a man presumed,—dared—to —to touch me with the end of his little finger. I would have suffered no man, king or prince, to have done what— what you did so easily—"

Suddenly she buried her face in both hands. I thought she was laughing at first.

"Don't touch me!" she sobbed,—ah! why don't I hate you!—why don't I— but I can't, I love you so much—so much!"

She would not suffer me to approach, much less to caress her. She sat there in the star-light, touching her eyes with her handkerchief and looking at the ground, until it was more than I could endure.

"I don't understand you, Lina," I said, "but I understand that when you are unhappy it breaks my heart. I will not say that I would die for you,—anybody, I fancy, would do that,—but I will say that if I live to come out of the Boznovian scrape, no woman in the world will have a husband who would live for her as I will live for you. It is easy to die for a woman you love ; it is easier to die for a woman who does not love in return ; but, if it were your pleasure, I would live forever in hell's torment to give you one moment's happiness."

When I delivered myself of this speech it did not seem silly or exaggerated. One can never tell what the most prosaic young man will say at times.

The effect however on Lina was curious. She sat up among the flowers, her slender body held very straight, her hands resting tightly against her breast. Something in her attitude made me think of arms and armour,—I don't know why, but I do know that she looked like a little princess receiving the homage due her, and I was proud and glad for her sake.

After a minute or two a change came over her ; she smiled and touched the lace on her apron.

" Your devotion is worthy of a maiden more nobly born," she said, with that almost indefinable tinge of irony in her voice. "I doubt if a serving-maid has ever before received such a splendid devotion as yours."

"I don't care what you are," I said. "If you are not noble, then it's the loss of the nobility. It's all nonsense to tell me that you have always been a lady's maid. I am not the sort of man that is attracted by inferiors."

"Shall I tell you who I am?" she asked suddenly.

"Is it not time?" I replied.

"Yes — no — yes — y-es. I am the orphan of well educated parents. I was well educated myself,—well enough, anyway to be chosen as companion to the Princess Sylvia of Marmora—"

"Witch Sylvia!" I exclaimed astounded.

"Yes. I read her books, I taught her to draw and paint, I tried to aid her to study. We tired of each other,—she grew weary of me, and I, at times, almost hated her. She was boisterous and feather-brained, she was shockingly unconventional.   She did silly daring things that brought her into contempt and ridicule. I sometimes pitied her, — she had no parents,—but I grew to loathe the very sight of her face.   I fear her too,—even now."

"You ? Why, Lina. You are with the Duchess, and the Duchess will be safe in schloss Lauterschnapps very soon."

"That would not keep Witch Sylvia from troubling me.   She used to torment me,—she bored me sometimes, and sometimes made me furious.   The mere sight of her disgusted me — ah, — you don't know what I've suffered from that woman !"

"You never will again if I come out of this all right," I said impetuously.   "I know what it must have been for a high-minded, sensitive woman like you to have been at the beck and call of an insolent, shallow, capricious, vixen like Witch Sylvia. Don't cry—Lina—why ! hello ! what's the matter ?"

She had sprung to her feet and stood silent, rigid, staring at me.   I also rose hastily and went toward her. As I approached she stepped back, then changing again swiftly she began to laugh, pressing one slender hand to her bosom.

"Do you know what you say?" she said, dropping again on the grass. "Do you not know that nothing on earth could protect me from Witch Sylvia—insolent, shallow, capricious, as you say she is,—if she chose to do me injury?"

"We'll see!" I said, tightening my lips; "this is the second time that I have heard how very terrible this Princess could be. I believe her own brother is afraid of her. I fancy however that when we enter Belgarde, the Princess Sylvia will not be visible. I wish, Lina, you would n't laugh and cry and do such abrupt things. I never can tell whether you are laughing or angry or what the mischief is the matter. If you are afraid of Witch Sylvia you need not be. Are you?"

"As I believe in the Sainted Virgin," said Lina slowly and earnestly, "I am afraid of this woman! And I know that you—I know that nobody in the whole world can keep her from harming me—if she wills to do it."

"Then let her beware!" said I passionately, "for I swear that if she does you injury she shall answer for it before all Europe."

"She shall answer for it to me," said Lina in a strange voice, "for now you have taught me not to fear her. I have loved her,—I have hated her, but I never shall fear her again. I said you were not to kiss me until we were married. I am mistress of myself and I choose to change my mind;—kiss me—and help me!"

In that swift caress I lost what senses I possessed. I held her in my arms,—she was so helpless and winning, so dependent, so child-like—and then, changing in a flash, she was a woman, passionate, proud of her love and her passion which seemed so new to her. Charming in her timidity, adorable in her innocent courage, human all through, she enchanted me, thrilled me, until the great wonder of it all overwhelmed me, and I trembled, faint with happiness too keen to bear.

At last she released my arm about her, and slipping her hand into mine, whispered that she must go.

"So soon?" I faltered.

"Yes.   Listen, I came here to beg you not to go with the King to conquer Boznovia.   I have listened to all you have said,—I have listened to the King and to the rest.   Believe me it cannot be done. Do you think that the spies have been idle? Do you imagine that all is not already known in Belgarde and in St. Petersburgh?   What chance has a stupid King like this one against Witch Sylvia who is determined that her brother shall keep his throne?   Believe me, she has not been idle. You may fill the pass with men and cannon instead of with silken cords, and that would not keep her spies away.   I know this woman ; you do not.   I know that you will fail—and yet— and yet I do not now ask you to turn back."

"I could not," I said gravely.

"That is why I do not ask it. You could not turn back honourably. But there is one thing I beg you to do. When the time comes and you march to Belgarde, I shall be working to help you,—to save you. I can do more than you think I can. And this is what I ask ; believe in me—in my love for you. No matter what you hear, no matter what you see, believe that I shall be secretly working for you. I shall leave the service of the Duchess the moment we arrive at the castle and I will help you,—don't laugh, my darling—I mean what I say."

"But—how can you, Lina ?"

"First by telling you to use your night-glass at once," she said gravely.

"My—my night-glass !" I stammered. I had completely forgotten the notch.

I raised the glasses nervously and then stood rigid.

A red star hung just above the scarred flank of the Osman Peak, twinkling, glimmering like a lamp—!—star ?—

"It 's the lantern," I whispered.

"Look,"said the girl—"how many ?"

"One—one—no ! there comes another ! There are two ! Lina, the strange man has gone out of the Tiflix valley !"

She came close to me and looked up into my startled eyes.

"You were never made for intrigue and violence," she said gently; "you are not even a good soldier. Sentinels keep watch, my darling, and of all places in the world the Balkans need watching. Listen again. I shall help you, for you need it. I shall enter Belgarde,—I shall enter the service of Witch Sylvia again. She would willingly take me back, although she will certainly misuse me if I allow it. But what do I care. I will keep you informed every day,—every hour if necessary. I will send you news by spies and messengers; I will warn you what roads to take and what to avoid. It is for your sake I do this. What do I care for this stupid King? It is only for you —my darling—only for your safety. For on your safety depends my happiness,— nay, my very life. Good night."

CHAPTER XII.

TWO weeks had passed but no sign or message came from either the Duke of Taxil in Paris or from General Bombwitz in Bazoùm.

The Duchess endured her captivity sullenly ; the King, worn with anxiety and the composition of proclamations, still bore up cheerfully. Every day the Duchess and Madge Grey walked in the woods with Mops ; his Grace of Babu, now reconciled to temperance and the Ispha nut, usually accompanied them. Whether the shock of his conversion had affected his scanty intelligence or whether the Ispha nut was responsible, I do not know, but his Grace of Babu suddenly developed a mania for writing verses. These verses he read aloud to us at breakfast. It was very depressing.

Obadiah also appeared to be unhappy. I sometimes imagined that the story of the Scripture bears bothered him for he left the strawberry vines untouched and never went out alone after dusk.   It was just as well.

Lina,—bless her little heart!—was the only one of us all who remained cheerful.

I often managed to see her alone.   In this the Duchess unwittingly aided me; for she had conceived an aversion to Lina, Heaven alone knows why!—and she never took her on her woodland prowls.   She took Mops however for which I trust I was sufficiently grateful. I had given the little pin, the gold Sainte-Catharine, to Lina, who promptly identified it as a gift to herself from the Princess Sylvia of Marmora.   She showed me the holy relic which it contained, the lock of hair from the head of Sainte-Catharine of Russia.   I asked her if she was not sceptical, considering the fact that the holy Sainte-Catharine had reddish gold hair and this lock of hair was black.   She said it made no difference in the value of the relic to her.   I quoted the case of the leopard and his spots, but she replied that hair and leopard spots could be changed when necessary.   I respect a faith like that.

In our stolen interviews she told me a great deal about her past life;—how it was she came to depend upon herself for her amusements, how she had patiently attempted to teach and amuse the Princess Sylvia, how they quarrelled with each other and then repented, only to quarrel again and again repent.

I learned a great deal about the blue-eyed, black-haired madcap, known all over Europe as Witch Sylvia.   Lina told me everything she knew and that was enough to give me an unpleasant idea of this selfish, capricious, beautiful dare-devil.

"If you see her you will surely fall in love with her, and then what shall I do?" said Lina one still evening while I kept my watch in the meadow.

"Do you think," said I scornfully, "that such a woman could interest me?"

"She is very charming," sighed Lina,

" she has wonderful soft silky black hair and—"

"I prefer golden hair," said I, glancing at her own.

" But black hair and blue eyes are a very beautiful combination ; don't you think so ?"

"No I don't," I replied, "especially when in conjunction with an empty selfish head."

"Ah," said Lina sadly ; "I have seen Witch Sylvia ; have you ? I have known her ; have you ? No man who ever saw her came away heart-whole and fancy-free. You cannot understand because you think that I, with my blond hair and blue eyes, am beautiful—"

"Think ! Anybody that denies that you are the most beautiful woman in the world is either wicked or crazy !"

She laughed, and blushed a little too.

"I shall never be sure that I have you until you have seen Witch Sylvia,—until you have been tried and proven," she said.

"I trust that I shall see her," I replied grimly.

"You will if you go to Belgarde."

"If I go? I will go!" I said carelessly. My carelessness did not deceive
Lina.

"You are worried," she said, touching
my hand caressingly. "Oh, I do wish
that your messenger would come. This
strain is telling on me too," she added
with a little sigh that went to my heart.

"They will come," I said trying to
speak bravely, "who knows but to-night,
—to-morrow, next day at latest, we shall
hear good news?"

"Who knows?" she repeated.

And so the evening wore away until
Lina crept into the house to sleep a little,
and I was left alone in the dusky meadow
with the stars overhead and the million
voices of the crickets ringing in my ears.

Along the edge of the dim glassy
meadow-pond, the water-fowl were sitting
huddled in rows, or standing motionless,
head buried, one foot lost in the down
of the breast. Myriads of daisies, pale,
snow flecks in the star-light, swayed with
every sudden zephyr. Faint spicy odors

came to me across the meadow from my garden, where roses and lilies nestled beneath their cloud of incense, where lilacs dripped with scented dew, and every little blossom poured out perfume to the high clustered stars.

And as I sat there, silent, wistful, dreaming such dreams as lovers know, far on the rim of the horizon a pale light flashed and the sudden night winds bore to me a sound, a murmur, indistinct, uncertain, vague as the whisper of the wind itself.

Motionless, breathless, I sat, my night-glass levelled on the horizon. Again from the darkness a pale flare lighted the clouds. I sprang to my feet, pausing a moment to listen; and again came the distant rumor, swelling as the zephyrs freshened, dying as they died.

In an instant I had crossed the road and entered the house. I sped through the dark hall-ways, rapping sharply at each door as I passed until I came to the King's chamber.

Here I knocked and entered without

ceremony, for the upper balcony lay under his window.

"Rise, your Majesty," I whispered, "there is something coming from the south,—wait,—you can see the light in the sky from the window!"

The King, only half awake, stumbled into his clothes and followed me out onto the balcony; and at the same moment, the Duchess appeared at the lower end of the balcony, swathed in a hideous tea-gown, a bed-quilt about her shoulders, a night-bonnet tied under her triple chin. One by one the others crept out, silent, shivering; Madge Grey, pale and quiet, Babu, round-eyed, stupid, munching an Ispha nut, Obadiah, Mops, and then, at last, came Lina, and her beautiful eyes met mine in the star-light and I saw her smile.

"What can it be!" said the King again and again, "I cannot understand those flashes of light. Can you, Mr. Steen?"

I shook my head nervously.

"Pardon,—if Majesty permits, I think I know," said Lina, and came forward, smiling and timid.

"What do you know?" boomed the Duchess contemptuously.

"Speak," said the King with an angry gesture toward the Duchess.

"It means,—this white light on the horizon,—that there is an army encamped there and that it is signalling to another army."

"Search lights!" exclaimed the King. "It must be that. I have never noticed them ;—I don't think my army had any—"

"Your army!" sneered the Duchess ; but she was very pale and her false teeth rattled in spite of her.

"My army was not supplied with anything modern, and the fault was mine," said the King mildly. "Lina, my child, —your name is Lina ?—yes ?—can you tell us anything more about these flashes ?"

"They are Morse signals," said Lina demurely ; "I studied telegraphy from necessity," she added with a smile.

"Can you read them then ?" I asked in some excitement.

"I will try—if Majesty permits—"

"Read—read, my child !" exclaimed the King—"look ! don't lose anything."

We stood breathless around her as she took my night-glasses and raised them. After a while she began to speak :

"Here is the first message at his Majesty's service; 'Push forward cavalry column to Ezrox Station. Seize railroad and material. Cut all wires toward Belgarde and the East.' Wait! now they are repeating the message; now it has been understood, and they resume—resume—ah : 'Throw First and Second Divisions of Tenth Corps into the Caspian Pass. Hold the Tiflix valley notch with Clisson's Hussar Guards'—"

"Clisson! Hurrah!" I shouted, "it's my regiment and the Caucasian army is here!"

How we cheered and shook hands,— and wept a little too, for, until now, we had scarcely realized the strain we had been under. Even Babu's face lighted up with something akin to intelligence, and he munched joyously on his Ispha nut, while the poor King, weak with emotion, pressed my hand again and again and leaned upon the balcony railing, tears of relief streaming down his worn face. Madge Grey and Lina, arm in arm, —for Madge seemed to forget the difference for a moment, bent over the King saying gentle, timid things to cheer him up. Obadiah seized Mops and dandled him and tossed him in an ecstasy of loyal fervor, neither heeding the snaps and shrieks of the cur nor the anathemas of the Duchess, until the one bit him and the other whacked him. Then he fled to the kitchen, from whence his mellow voice rose in songs of praise. The Duchess alone of all the company remained stolid and insensible, her stony face turned toward the King. But all the same I could see that it was only her fat-headed brutish malevolence, that prevented her from expressing the relief and satisfaction that she felt.

At an order from me, Obadiah reappeared with refreshments and we all nibbled on lettuce sandwiches and cold chicken, while I kept the glasses levelled on the flashes, and Lina, standing close to my shoulder, read them for us all.

Somewhere behind the Caspian range, a great army was moving in two divisions, and it was moving northward toward Belgarde. Some of the messages we understood, some we did not, for the King was woefully deficient in military knowledge, and, as for me, I began to realize my appalling ignorance now that the hour had struck.

After a while the Duchess retired, sullenly demanding Lina's aid, for she announced, that, as the army had come, she could secure horses to get back to castle Lauterschnapps. So Lina went away to pack the shapeless wardrobe of her Grace, and Babu fell asleep with his mouth open, and Madge, the King, and I were left to watch the stars flicker out in the heavens, and the mist and smoke that hung over the invisible army grow greyer and pinker as the east flushed with the coming dawn.

It was about three o'clock in the morning, I believe, when Madge touched my arm and pointed to a dark spot on the hill where the high-road disappears against the sky.   Nearer and nearer it came, and now we could see that it was a body of horsemen, galloping swiftly, — hundreds of them,—a full regiment of cavalry. The white dust hung above them, behind them, and drifted away along either flank, as they galloped nearer and ever nearer. Now we could see their horses' heads tossing and jerking, now we could see the scarlet jackets of the riders, flashes of bit and spur and scabbard, while · the dull shock of iron-shod hoofs grew, increasing like advancing surf, until the road below us shook with the coming host and the hills rang back the clash of steel.   Right past the house they thundered, shrouded in clouds of dust ; then the shrill trumpet notes pierced the air, the long column wheeled, wavered, backed, and halted, facing the house.   A heavy voice broke into the sudden calm ; other voices echoed the command from end to end of the restless line.   Swish ! swish ! swis—sh ! A thousand sabres swept from their scabbards of steel, a thousand red sleeves shot into the air, a thousand voices crashed out :

"Health to the King!"

The pale colour in the King's face deepened. He took one unsteady step forward.

"Go down," I whispered.

Stumbling, uncertain, his Majesty descended the outer steps, and I saw his hands trembling along the balustrade.

Two officers hurried forward saluting. One was the Duke of Taxil, the other was Clisson. The King held out his hand, then both arms. Taxil flopped into them.

When Clisson caught sight of me he pulled his grey moustache and winked. I went down to him and fell upon his neck. This manœuvre gave me an opportunity to whisper :

"Clisson for Heaven's sake run this regiment for me until I can learn how to handle it. You are lieutenant-colonel from this moment. Conceal the ignorance of your colonel from the men and I'll make you anything you wish when we get to Belgarde."

They had brought me my colonel's uniform and equipment and I sent a trooper with it to my room.

"There is no time to waste I know," said I, shaking hands with Taxil and Bombwitz, "we read your signals last night and we know you are bound for the Tiflix notch and the station at Ezrox."

Clisson stared at this display of military acumen.   It pleased me.

I called Obadiah, gave him some whispered orders, and hastened to my room. Here I put on the scarlet astrakan edged dolman, the black, scarlet-striped riding breeches, the spurred boots, and the hussars busby.   In a few moments my sabre was snapped to the clasp, my revolver and binocular slung from shoulder to hip, and my steel chin-chain tightened.

The Duchess sneered a little as I went to her to make my adieus, but Madge Grey gave me both her hands and said some very sweet things.

"We leave under escort in half an hour.   We have decided to go by way of Bazoum," she said.   "Shall we meet in Belgarde?"

"Yes," I said.

Then we bade each other farewell, very quietly and simply.

In the library I found Lina alone. She was a trifle pale when I took her into my arms.

"Remember," she said, "I will help you and save you. Heed every messenger, every message I send you."

"I will," I said passionately.

"Then Heaven keep you," she said firmly; "I cannot live if you are killed."

"I won't be killed," I muttered.

"You shall not be," she cried.

"In Belgarde, then," I groaned, crushing her to me.

"In Belgarde," she repeated.

She pinned the gold Sainte-Catharine to my dolman. A tear fell from her lashes onto my hand.

"Beware Witch Sylvia," she murmured, trying to smile.

I touched her hand with my lips, and at the same moment the Duchess waddled into the room.

For a moment we looked at her amazed

face, then I bent again and kissed Lina's beautiful fingers.

"You will leave my service as soon as we reach schloss Lauterschnapps!" shouted the Duchess. "Do you understand!"

I kissed Lina again, on the lips.

"My darling," I said, "I have ordered an ein-spänner and an escort. Obadiah shall accompany you and Constantine shall drive you to Zitlis. There you are to take Obadiah and the train and go to Belgarde by way of Bazoum. Your little valise is already in the ein-spänner. Constantine gives you his daughter as maid—"

"That's my maid!" cried the Duchess furiously. "How dare you!—" I drew Lina's arm through mine.

"Come," I said, "this old lady is losing her temper." And I led her out through the garden to the barn where Obadiah and Constantine stood, holding the horse. Zilka, Constantine's red cheeked daughter sat on the trunk behind.

"Constantine," said I, "I have already told you that I am entrusting my fiancée to your care. Obadiah, every kink on your head will answer for this lady's safety. Zilka, my child, be faithful." Then I aided Lina to mount the vehicle.

"Keep Obadiah," said I, "until I come to claim you in Belgarde. Here is what you will need for your journey. It is in gold." She looked at the money in a startled way. Tears filled her eyes and she leaned out and flung both arms around my neck.

In another moment I had motioned to Constantine, the vehicle whirled away, and five troopers from the stables mounted and clattered after it.

After a while I turned from the distant dust cloud and went through the garden to the pheasantry. Here Georgiades joined me and I gave him the keys of the house and stables.

"Keep the place in order ; feed the creatures and use the garden as your own. If the Servian Government confiscates the place as it will if it learns that I am mixed up in this affair, here is money enough to repay you. If the Servian

Government does not seize it, I will re-turn unless I am shot. Good-bye."

As I finished I saw General Bombwitz and the King come into the garden and beckon to me. I went to them and told them that I was ready. The King wore his uniform, silver helmet and all.

They brought our horses and we mounted and cantered out to the road and along the long lines of cheering troopers. I looked appealingly at Clisson and raised my gloved hand. He saluted gravely, swung his horse and bellowed an order that set the trumpets clanging a frenzied summons.

" Forward ! Trot ! Gallop !" he bawled, and the Hussars of the Guard thundered on toward the Tiflix notch.

CHAPTER XIII.

IT was five o'clock in the morning when we galloped into the notch and drew bridle. So hot had been our pace that I had scarcely time for a breathless word or two with Clisson. Now at a signal from me, the trumpets rang " dismount," and a thousand saddles were emptied as though by magic.

Clisson detailed one troop armed with carbine and lance, to hold the narrow pass. I thought to myself that half a troop would be sufficient to keep ten thousand in check in the Tiflix notch, but I looked wise and said nothing. The King, followed by Bombwitz and Taxil, rode up, urging the immediate direction of a mountain battery to the further end of the pass. Clisson replied that machine guns and in-

.fantry were on the way and pointed to my house in the valley below where already a battalion of cyclist infantry was mounting.

"The guns are coming as quickly as the mules can trot," he added; "we have the pass now anyway and we must push on to Ezrox and secure the railway. If your Majesty will step to the point of rock above, I can explain." As he spoke he drew a bundle of maps from the breast of his dolman, selected one, unfolded it and led the way to the flat table-rock which dominated the pass.

With a stem of wild-oats, he began tracing routes and rivers and railroads on his map, spread flat on the rock, four stones on each corner to keep it from being blown away by the wind. And all the time he was rattling on, gesticulating, now and then referring to his Major, a keen eyed, sun-scorched Frenchman who nodded and chewed a straw.

Taxil and Babu, brilliant in their crimson dolmans and glittering spurs, paid the greatest attention to Clisson's harangue.

So did the King, leaning heavily on General Bombwitz' arm. As for me I followed him easily, partly because I had already studied the region near Ezrox, partly, perhaps, because I understood Parisian French better than the others did.

When Clisson finished he looked at me interrogatively.

"How much rest do the horses need?" I asked.

"An hour," he said, "we galloped hard through the star-light this morning. We have time to picket them."

"See here old fellow," I said, drawing him aside, "do what you think best. What the devil do I know about cavalry or anything else!" Clisson's left eyelid fluttered gently, but he saluted me and tramped away, followed by a dismounted trumpeter.

The King, leaning on the arm of General Bombwitz, had stepped into the open door of Constantine's hut, a low, white plaster building, half sheltered by the cliff. His Grace of Babu followed them but Taxil strolled up to me, twisting his waxed moustache and lifting his sabre over the stony road.

"Have I done well?" he asked.

"Indeed you have!" I exclaimed warmly.

"And when we get back to Belgarde am I to have the railroad from my mines?"

"Certainly.   There is one thing however that I do not understand and that is, why you neither wrote me from Bazoum nor sent me any messengers.   I thought you understood what I told you."

"Messengers!" said Taxil, astonished, "why I sent you three!"

"They never arrived," I replied, much troubled; "ten to one they were in the pay of Russia."

"Or Witch Sylvia," he added nervously. "I tried my best,—I employed men picked from the best.   You can never be certain of any man in the Balkans.   The last messenger I sent you was escorted to the south end of the Tiflix valley by my cavalry patrol to make certain.   He entered the valley, and I don't see how he could have gotten out without your knowledge."

I thought of the mysterious Russian who had left the valley at night but said nothing to Taxil about it.

"Well," said I, " you may imagine how nervous his Majesty was. As for me, I tell you I was more than unhappy. But it's all right now; we have the pass and we'll hold the railroad before noon. Did you have any difficulty in finding Clisson? What did the King of Caucasia say and where is his army and—tell me something about the state of affairs! I have n't an idea about anything."

"The King of Caucasia is in the field with a hundred thousand men. His right wing lay on the Zitlis hills last night, his left wing, to the cavalry division of which your regiment is attached, is swinging along a line, twenty miles front, gradually concentrating by columns at Ezrox. I know very little about the movement of the centre. I believe the King of Caucasia expects to seize all the Caspian passes, force the passage of the Ulma at

Kerestan, turn Dragovitza by a flank movement, and over-run Biznitz. That of course would mean the capitulation of Belgarde."

"Oh yes," I assented, trying to under- stand. It appeared that even the venal and incapable Duke of Taxil knew some things that I did n't. I was slowly com- ing to the conclusion that my proper place was in some awkward squad or possibly in a minor cadet school.

"I 'm no soldier, that 's apparent," thought I to myself, and looked gloomily at Taxil.

"The King of Caucasia sent money by messengers to our own King," said the Duke. "Did he not receive anything?"

"Not a pfenning!" I replied, turning to look at the King who was now emerg- ing from the house, followed by General Bombwitz and the Duke of Babu.

At the same moment Clisson ran up saying, "Hasten, gentlemen, mount!" and the bugles in the pass rang "boots-and- saddles."

Far down the pass I could see the head

of a column moving up behind our dismounted troopers. It was composed of cyclist infantry, dismounted, escorting a mule-battery.

Ten minutes later Clisson and I were riding side by side, and behind us crowded the long winding column of the Hussar Guard, King and standards in the centre, surrounded by a picked squadron commanded by Bombwitz, Taxil, and his Grace of Babu.

" Ha! " chuckled Clisson, twisting his gray moustache, " I think we need not be ashamed of our red riders, eh ! Steen ?"

Then, at my request he told me how he had worked to drum up all his old comrades of the Chasseurs d'Afrique ; how ninety nine per cent jumped at the chance ; how he had also secured enough relics from the Foreign Legion to make an even thousand ; Italians, Russians, Americans, English, even Turks and needy gentlemen representing almost every country of Europe. " It's a devil of a regiment," he grinned. " We rendezvoused in Bazoum, and when I had them uniformed and mounted, the King of Caucasia swore the whole regiment into his service with the pledge that, on the surrender of Belgarde and the restoration of King Theobald, the regiment should return to Bazoum as a corps d'élite of the Horse-Guards. You need n't worry about our pay either ; we 're already paid in advance for the few days this campaign will last, and we have a big bounty awaiting us in Bazoum."

As we rode on, side by side, I asked him to describe this King of Caucasia, and he did, as only a Frenchman can do such things, in four words ; " Fat, freckled, practical, prosaic."

"I knew that he 'd help our King on promise of a free port of entry for his commerce and his two torpedo boats. He 'll build more boats now ; he 'll unload all his productions on Austria and Germany and make a pretty penny. I suppose he has lead mines ?"

"Lots," laughed Clisson, patting his horse's neck with his gloved hand.

"Pleasant prospect for Boznovia," I said, and turned in my saddle to look at the column.   I could not see his Majesty's face or figure but the tall silver helmet, with its gold winged griffin, towered among the busbys of the troopers, flashing and scintillating in the morning sunlight.

"I should think, Clisson," said I, "that his Majesty's helmet was as good as a heliograph to warn an enemy of our presence."

"Of course it's all fol-de-rol!" muttered Clisson, "but what can you expect in Boznovia?"

We rode for awhile in silence, listening to the rhythmic trample of the horses behind us, the clatter of lance and carbine, and the jingling of chain, bit, and spur.

I wondered a little that we had passed no Servian gendarmes, or frontier guards. Even at the Tiflix notch where the three kingdoms come to a triangular centre, I had seen no Servians. As for the other countries, this frontier of Boznovia and Caucasia is too savage and wild to need watching, for even the smugglers shun it, the Tiflix valley being the only possible approach to Ezrox. The valley was considered a neutral highway by the Treaty of Vienna in 1874, although Servia claimed it as part of her territory, agreeing only to its use as a neutral highway on this condition.

When we left the pass we entered Boznovia, using the neutral highway between Caucasia and the Boznovian frontier. Servia might have objected had she had time to seize the pass.

I told Clisson this and he wondered why they had not done so.

" We should have lost a week; I 'm glad they did n't," I said.

" Servia is acting queerly it seems to me," observed Clisson ; " they must know what is going on,—they must have known it long ago. Russia also has made no movement, and it seems strange, does n't it ? "

" You expected a battle here at the pass ? " I asked curiously.

" Why of course. The King of Caucasia never expected to get through the Caspians without a tussle with Servia."

"What !" I exclaimed, "you expected to fight Servia, also ?"

"Why, " said Clisson, coolly, " did n't you ?"

"No,—I never thought of that," I replied.

"Did n't the King, either ?" demanded Clisson in amazement.

"I suppose not," I answered sulkily.

Then Clisson began to chuckle and banter me and torment me until I retorted indignantly :

"How the devil can you expect a simple civilian to think of all these complications? I certainly forgot to take Servia into consideration—but I could n't think of everything, could I ?"

"But," laughed Clisson," the Servians have just walloped the Boznovians to please Russia. Is n't it reasonable to expect that they would also attempt to wallop the Caucasians if Russia gave them the wink? And we are going to reinstate the very King that Russian intrigue chased out of Belgarde ! And we are going to chase the Marmora Prince, whom Russia placed there, back to his penny principality again ! My ! how diplomatic you are !"

" Nonsense," said I, half laughing, half angry : "if Servia moves, Bulgaria is with us. If Russia moves, England, Austria, and Italy are with us. If France lifts a finger, Germany, Roumania, and all Asia are behind us."

" Don't you believe it," said Clisson ; but I saw that he had been joking me, and that he himself believed it.

" The simple fact is this," I observed ; " we have struck a spark that may set the world ablaze. If one country, no matter how small, takes sides with either contestant in this coming duel, it means a universal war that will necessitate a change in public school geographies."

And so we rode on through the flowering plain, speculating, insisting, disputing until our advanced guard came galloping back in a shower of dust and pebbles to report that the Ezrox station was in sight.

" I 'm going out with the advance," I cried eagerly, "do you mind, Clisson ?"

"It's damned unmilitary," he muttered, "to see a Colonel go scuttling out with the vedettes." Then, catching the fun of the thing, he laughed and beckoned to a dozen troopers.

"We 'll carry it by assault," he chuckled to me, "come on!" and we struck spurs to our horses and flew out along the road at full speed.

Almost immediately we sighted the white stone station lying silent and deserted in the bright June sunshine.

On we raced, bending low in our saddles, sabres clanking, revolvers poised, the lance-pennants of our escort flapping and snapping in the wind.

"Empty!" cried Clisson, pulling up sharply at the edge of the platform where the long lines of glistening rails swept in a splendid curve around the base of the hill.

I dismounted, and the escort tumbled out of their saddles, carbines unslung.

I shoved my revolver back into the holster, walked to the closed door, and rapped.

"It 's deserted, is n't it ?" called Clisson.

"Hark !" cried a trumpeter, leaping back, "there is something inside that house !" and he sounded the "alert" with all the strength of his lungs.

"Look out !" shouted Clisson, drawing his sabre, "I saw something pass that second window !"

"Then in with the door !" I cried, and flung myself full weight against it. It gave way easily and I sprang in and levelled my revolver at a dark figure in a corner behind a table.

"Prisoner !" shouted the troopers, crowding into the dim room.

A yell of laughter burst from Clisson who had followed, and at the same moment a great mustard-coloured bear reared up from behind the table, and made toward us waving his paws.

"Don't fire !" gasped Clisson weak with laughter, "he 's got a collar on and a ring in his nose !"

The troopers drew back in confusion ; the bear looked appealingly at Clisson.

"This is terrible," I said, scarlet with mortification, for I heard the rest of the regiment galloping up outside. But Clisson, tears of mirth streaming down his bronzed cheeks, seized a lance from a trooper and thrust it into the bear's paws. "Dance!" he cried, and the bear pricked up his ears and waltzed gravely toward us.

"Come on!" commanded Clisson, "allons! en avant!" and the bear waltzed out of the house and over the platform in full view of the entire regiment.

"Prisoner!" shouted the men, and a roar of laughter rose from the ranks while the horses snorted and reared and the lances rattled in the stirrups.

Then the King galloped out and faced the regiment.

"Soldiers!" he cried in a mighty voice, "the Russian bear shall dance to the same tune!"

Then the troopers swung their sabres and cheered and the trumpets played the Boznovian "Salute to the King," while the bear, a trifle astonished, leaned on his lance shaft and gazed admiringly at the King. As for me I was profoundly mortified.

"If you ever tell—!" I muttered as Clisson passed me.

He was too much exhausted with laughter to reply.

CHAPTER XIV.

THAT night his Majesty slept on a wooden bench in the Ezrox railroad station and the troopers slept under the stars.

About ten o'clock I went out with Clisson to make the rounds. We passed along the lines of picketed horses, crossed the railroad tracks, and walked slowly from post to post, while from every side came the sharp challenges and the rattle of carbines, or the stamp and snort of horses. Far down the tracks, along the glimmering lines of rails, the vedettes stood against the sky, carbines poised, motionless save when the horses tossed their heads or a star-beam struck some breeze lifted pennon or sparkling lance-tip.

15

A new moon, slim and keen as a sabre blade, flashed among the stars ; and over all the still fragrant night spread a vast veil, mysterious, filmy, vague as the veil of Isis. Behind us the massed foliage of a forest rose, while on either side meshed branches and slim trees bordered the sky with lace-work. All around the pastures lay embroidered with dim sweet blossoms, pale blots in the gloom, and from hollow and hill-side, from meadow and sward, the song of the crickets swelled unceasing.

"Fichtre !" said Clisson, prosaic and practical to the last, "there's fodder enough for the whole cavalry division in that pasture,—yes, and for the train-des-equipages too. What a pity we human creatures are unable to appreci-ate a good grass supper !"

"Bother take you Clisson," said I, "can't you enjoy the night without count-ing horses' noses?" I had been dream-ing of Lina.

"Zut !" said the hussar, "I 've other things to occupy me ; so have you, mon ami,—sacré nom d'un nom !—what's that !"

"What? Oh—that's the bear.   He'll scare the vedettes and get a hide full of lead in a moment."

"Confound the brute," said Clisson, "a shot might turn the whole camp upside down ! I wish you'd be more careful in your selection when you make any more of the enemy prisoners."

"Don't try to be funny," said I, "I'll get the bear back myself ;" and I ran down the path and seized the great crea-ture by the collar.

"Come," said I angrily, "you've made me ridiculous enough for one day," and I dragged on the collar with all my strength. The bear was very docile,—even deprecat-ingly servile.   He trundled along beside me anxiously, and acknowledged Clisson's presence by sitting up and waving his paws.

"I don't believe there's a growl left in him," said Clisson.   "We can't keep him with our cavalry you know; we must attach him to headquarters."

"Officially!"

"Yes," said Clisson with a grave gesture, "he is the private property of King Theobald of Boznovia."

"What shall we name him?" I asked.

"I don't know,—he looks a little like the Metropolitan Aloysius of Belgarde—"

"He looks more like Babu," I suggested.

"So he does!" assented Clisson, "but that won't do my son. We could call him Daniel,—Daniel, in the bear's den,—don't you know."

"Lion's den," I observed.

"It's all the same. Daniel, sit up! See, he minds very well. We really should name him Daniel. Shall we?" Before I could reply, a vedette's quick challenge rang from the extreme outposts.

"Hark!" said Clisson, " do you hear that!"

A dull sound came to our ears, the rythmic movement of marching men, and, as we listened, the distant trampling cadence grew and grew until I saw, through the darkness, a long misty column looming up across the meadows with the shimmer of bayonets above.

On they came, the star-light vibrating on the tossing bayonets, tramp, tramp, tramp, across the railroad and down along the meadow to the little river behind the willows.

" It 's Vladina's division," said Clisson, " see the double white cross on their caps ! "

" Count Vladina of Bazoum ? "

" Yes.   It 's his Foot-Guards that are passing.   Well, the army is coming, you see, and I suppose we must be up and off before daylight." He yawned unaffectedly and looked at me.

" Come on to bed then," I said, and we turned away toward the Ezrox station.

" The King of Caucasia is with the centre, or was last night.   He may be here by morning," said Clisson,—"hold on,—keep that bear from walking on my boots ! "

" Daniel ! " I cried sternly, " walk on your own toes."

As we rounded the railway curve below

the hill, another column wheeled into view, more infantry, while from the high-road came the creaking of baggage wagons and the tinkle-clink-clank of moving artillery.   The whole plain was in motion now.   In they crept, long dim columns, now indistinct, now visible when a turn of the flank set the star-light dancing across the broad billows of bayonets.

At last we came to the railroad station and entered, the challenge of the vedette ringing in our ears.   The King was awake and demanded to know whether the King of Caucasia had arrived.   We told him all we knew and passed on to the outer office, the bear following.   Clisson threw himself on a pile of over-coats, inviting me to share the couch, but I sat down in a chair by the empty fire-place and in two minutes was asleep.

I awoke at intervals through the night, listening to the movement and the mighty murmur of the passing host, hour after hour, but I always fell asleep again, to dream fitfully.   Strange faces haunted my dreams, sometimes the face of Lina, sometimes the face of a fiend peering at me from a veil of black hair, until I cried out and stumbled to my feet, my ears singing with the reveillé from the silver throated trumpets.   Clisson also rose yawning and stretching, his sabre clashing with every movement; and the bear trudged around the room sniffing at the cracks under the doors where the fresh sweet country breeze entered.   We let him out, and Clisson called to Farron, the battalion Adjutant to see that Daniel was fed.

Dawn was already coming up behind the Caspian mountains; the air smelled fresh and aromatic, and the grass before our door hung low, drenched with dew.   I went to the door and looked out.   What a change had come during the night! Everywhere, as far as the eye could reach, dark masses of troops were in motion, cavalry, infantry, endless jumbles of baggage and provision wagons; and everywhere bugles were summoning the drowsy, echoing cheerily over the meadows, while on the edge of the woods the cavalry trumpets chorussed a mellow symphony, and the deep drums rolled from the valley below.

I heard Clisson's brisk voice, now explaining some detail to the King, now receiving the Veterinary-Surgeon's report, now chatting with the Major and the Quartermaster-Sergeant, or sharply rebuking a wrangling battalion farrier and a quarrelsome stable Sergeant. There had been no casualties during the night except that an artificer had got drunk and punched a wagoner in the nose.

The trumpeters were playing the salute to the colours before I finished a hasty toilet in the corner sink, and joined the mess in the large waiting office. The King appeared to be in better spirits now. He laughed at the antics of Daniel who had smelled out the sugar and was pawing the air in mute supplication.

Taxil and Babu came in, hungry and full of accounts concerning the corps that had been arriving during the night and was still passing.

"The Duke of Etropolis is in command," said Taxil, swallowing a bowl of tea, "but I can't find either him or Count Vladina."

"The guards did n't halt," observed Clisson ; "we shall pass them on our way to Ravno.   What cavalry is that over by the woods ? "

"Prince Saranitza's dragoons," replied Taxil ; "they are to wait there for General Brimborio's division of infantry. What is our first halting place, Colonel Clisson ?"

"Ravno, a village on the Demsa ; our next is Vistmark on the same stream and then we arrive at Tchatal-Dagh."

"From Tchatal-Dagh we can see Belgarde," I added.

A pale flush touched the King's face. He pushed back his chair and rose, assisted by Taxil and Clisson.   I heard the trumpets playing the "Salute to the King" as they went out into the meadow and presently I followed them, leading Daniel by the collar.   There was a colour-sergeant passing, and I gave Daniel into his hands with strict orders to make him comfortable in the ambulance.

Ten minutes later the Hussar Guards,

trumpets sounding, standards and guidons fluttering, trotted out of the meadow by the Ezrox station and wheeled into the Ravno high-way. The King, as before, rode in the centre with Taxil, Babu, and General Bombwitz, surrounded by the standard bearers and the picked guards. Clisson and I and the chief-trumpeter rode on well ahead.

We passed several battalions of Vladina's infantry by the river bank in the valley but we saw nothing of the Count himself. Farther along we came upon an artillery train in motion, and beyond that an interminable line of baggage wagons escorted by Bazoum lancers and cyclist infantry.

Across the railroad another train was moving, also escorted by cavalry, and from every hill, flag signals were being exchanged, heliographs flashed in the first sunbeams, and long lines of field-telephone wire were being hung, stretching from tree to tree away back to the Ezrox station which I now concluded was to become an important base of supply.

The railroad tracks were heavily patrolled by lancers and by chasseurs à cheval of the Curtina regiment, gay troopers in orange and light blue.

Our own red riders attracted universal attention, part of which was certainly due to the towering griffin-crowned silver helmet of the King. The Caucasian troops evidently recognized him for, whenever we passed a regiment, the drums gave the nine ruffles, the bugles pealed the " Salute to the King," and the standards swept the ground. These marching salutes were very pleasant to the King, poor monarch !—he had been drummed out of Boznovia to a very different tune. Taxil also seemed pleased. Babu's round face was expressionless and emotionless except when he gravely chewed on his eternal Ispha nuts.

Clisson, bubbling over with satisfaction and good spirits, eulogized his regiment and gave me the personal history of so many of his old comrades that I became completely muddled and begged him to stop. At ten o'clock we walked our horses into the hamlet of Ravno, where we watered them and made inquiries, surrounded by stupid staring Boznovian peasants. Then we took up our line of march again. At noon we passed through Vistmark, crossing the river by the ancient stone bridge, but seeing no signs of opposition or of sullen unwillingness among the village people. Nobody, however, cheered for the King which fact I remarked to Clisson.

When we moved out of Vistmark, our advanced guard was cautioned, for we were approaching Tchatal-Dagh.

It was one o'clock precisely when the bang! bang! of cavalry carbines touched up the regiment like an electric shock. In a few minutes our advanced guard came pelting back, reporting heavy masses of infantry on the hills in front.

Clisson and I spurred forward until we came to a hill, crowned by the hamlet of Dragovitza. We could see a few of the enemy's cavalry, moving about the hilltop, silhouetted against the sky, but at first we discovered no infantry. Clisson found them before I did.

"Good Lord!" he exclaimed, "will you look at that plateau, Steen!"

I turned my glasses on the table-land indicated.   It was black with heavy masses of infantry and artillery.   Beyond, the spires and minarettes of Tchatal-Dagh glistened in the sun like icicles, and all around them the heavy pine forests lay, stretching away to the wall of the Black Fortress of Tchenekoi, the gate of Belgarde.

"There is an army there," said Clisson, "and probably most of it is lying under cover of the pine woods.   Surely they don't mean to offer us battle here; that would be too absurd when they could have the support of the Black Fortress if they wanted it."

The enemy's cavalry pickets, numbering possibly fifty, were galloping toward us by this time, so we wheeled and trotted back to our main body.

Clisson dispatched messengers and aids to find Count Vladina and the Duke of Etropolis.   He also sent messengers to General Brimborio and to the colonel of the last artillery regiment that we had passed. Cyclist infantry had begun to arrive at the front and we utilized these swift messengers also, and to such good purpose that in half an hour Vladina's van-guard came into sight, followed by the Bazoum lancers, six mounted batteries of artillery, and Prince Saranitza's dragoons. Orders also came, from the Duke of Etropolis, to retire and take up our position on a hill which rose behind us, commanding the entire valley and table-land beyond Dragovitza.

At a sign from Clisson the trumpets sounded and we wheeled our horses' into the fields to the right, cutting a broad swathe through the sun-dried grass and daisies. A mounted battery, a few yards away, kept abreast of us, the limbers and bronze field-pieces plunging through the meadow grass up to the wheel-hubs, the horses straining under the polished creak-ing harness. Beneath our horses feet the springy sod shook as we cantered across the grass, leaving long trails of crushed poppies, red as blood. In a few minutes we were crashing through a young maize field, over crackling stalks and innocent blue corn-flowers, putting to flight flock after flock of wrens and hedge-birds.

Up the slope we toiled, the loose earth and pebbles falling as our horses' steel-shod hoofs broke into the soft soil; and at length we rode over the last incline and galloped out across a stony plateau, all covered with tufts of yellow broom and Russian thistles.

Already a field-battery had unlimbered on the edge of the hill; the horses were being lead away to the hollow below, and the covers of the ammunition chests were flying open, click! click! while a Major of artillery followed by a bugler, walked up and down bellowing orders and rattling his sabre hilt fiercely.

Other batteries were arriving as we wheeled again and trotted into a little hollow to the right, sheltered by a thicket of poplar trees.

Here our troopers dismounted, flinging themselves on the ground beside a clear cold brook that flowed swiftly through copse, but Clisson and I followed the King up the slope again toward a group of officers who had just galloped up to the batteries and were examining the valley below.

"Zut!" said Clisson, "there are the Count Vladina and the Duke of Etropolis!"

"Yes," said the King quietly, "and I think I see the King of Caucasia also."

At that moment one of the officers caught sight of us and, hastily dismounting came toward the King, both hands outstretched.

It was King Casimir of Caucasia.

"See 'em embrace!" sneered Clisson aside to me, as the two monarchs fell into each other's arms, "every hug that old Casimir gives means, 'I 've got you now and you 've got to let my ships into the Balkan Sea'; and every squeeze that our King gives in return means, 'only get me into Belgarde and you can do what you d—n please!'"

"You 're a cynical Frenchman," said I, "it 's a very affecting sight,—hello! here comes the staff to be presented ; buck up and look interested if you can—" Before I could finish we were in the centre of a throng of brilliantly uniformed officers bowing and saluting and returning compliments and pledges until Taxil, Babu, and Bombwitz came up and created a diversion of interest from ourselves. Prince Saranitza, gorgeous in his dragoon's uniform, slipped his arm through mine and dragged me away to inspect the plateau beyond ; and the others followed the two sovereigns toward a marquee which was pitched behind the hillside on the banks of the clear meadow brook.

"There must be thirty or forty thousand infantry in those woods over there," said Prince Saranitza, levelling his fieldglasses. "I suppose they expect us to attack and I hope we will, don't you ?"

"I don't know anything about it," I replied frankly, also bringing my glasses to bear on the plateau.

"We none of us do except the King and the Duke of Etropolis," observed the Prince,—"by the way, you 've got a fine cavalry brigade ; I saw them in Bazoum and also this morning before you started.   With my dragoons and a regiment or two from Plotz's division, we ought to have a jolly good charge,—now don't you think so ? "

" Oh yes," said I, " of course I want to try something of that sort when the time comes.   What do you suppose the King of Caucasia will do ? "

" It looks as if he was massing the artillery to shell them out of the woods and then charge them with Vladina's infantry. We will probably be sent after them when they run."

" *If* they run," said I.

" Exactly," laughed the Prince, " and of course they will, you know.   Won't it be fun to go clattering along on their heels right up to the gates of Belgarde."

" Indeed it will be," said I, " but what about the Black Fortress of Tchenekoi ? "

" Storm it," said Saranitza cheerfully, —" hello, here comes Clisson."

" The King of Caucasia gives us permission to take a few men and ride to Dragovitza for information," said Clisson, saluting.

"Come on then," cried the Prince, motioning to a trooper who was holding his horse; and in a moment Clisson, the Prince, and I, followed by an escort of our red riders, were galloping along the rear of the batteries, exchanging salutes and merry badinage with passing artillery officers. In a minute or two we arrived again at the slope. Through the trampled cracking maize stalks and out into the meadow we galloped until we came to the Ravno highway, where the engineers were fortifying the stone bridge that spans the meadow stream.

"Be cautious," said Clisson; "we found the enemy's cavalry roaming about that hilltop when we came in. sight of Dragovitza before."

"We could drive them out with our peloton," suggested the Prince.

"Certainly," replied Clisson sarcastically, "but that's exactly what we did n't come for."

The Prince laughed and spurred forward with a careless gesture to me, and we all followed at a hand-gallop. I thought I heard Clisson mutter "idiot," but I was not sure.

In a dozen rods we suddenly came in sight of the hamlet of Dragovitza, and Clisson drew bridle and called sharply to the Prince.

"Slowly, slowly now; we don't want to ride down a regiment by mistake; it might stampede them, you know."

"There is n't a horseman in sight," said I, "perhaps the road is clear—"

"—And perhaps it is n't," said Clisson, peering through his field-glasses; "come on anyway, and remember we are not looking for a belly-full of bullets just yet."

I turned to the troopers of the peloton and ordered them to sheath sabres and unsling their carbines. Clisson drew his revolver and examined the cylinder carefully, but Prince Saranitza bared his dragoon's sabre with a laugh.

"Arme-blanche for me," he said, " I

prefer it " ; and we gathered our bridles and trotted up the hill in open order.

" Look out ! " sang out Clisson, " there 's something moving behind that cow-shed to the left ! " Without a word the Prince put his horse to the road-side ditch and made straight for the shed.

" Come back ! " shouted Clisson, and then, cursing, jumped his horse over the same ditch and followed the feather-brained dragoon. At the same moment the rattle of carbines broke out from the village and the bullets came zip ! ztzing ! z——zt ! around our ears.

A light veil of smoke hung across the single village street, and through it I caught a glimpse of mounted forms, scurrying away toward the highway beyond.

" There are only a dozen of them ! " I cried, and galloped into the village, followed by my peloton of hussars. It was deserted except for a frightened chicken that rushed headlong into a weed patch, squawking. Saranitza and Clisson came up at the same moment. I sent my men through every hut, every barn-yard, to find a native, but all the huts were empty, and we pushed on, carbines and revolvers poised.

When we came to the end of the village, we could plainly see, far down the white highway, the cloud of dust kicked up by the enemy's flying vedettes.

"They are making tracks for the plateau and the woods," said the Prince; "shall we give them a race?"

Clisson disdained to answer him, but, dismounting, sat down on a rock and raised his field-glasses. We followed his example.

Far on the edge of the plain the towers and minarettes of Tchatal-Dagh glistened in the sun-light; to the east the dense pine forests of Boznovia swept in a semi-circle about the plateau; to the west the Caspian Mountains shimmered blue and ponderous, and below us lay the valley of the Demsa, green and fresh under a cloudless sky. We could discover no troops in the valley, but the dark masses of infantry still lay along the edge of the forest on the plateau.

It was noon, and Clisson produced a bottle of red wine and some Servian cheese, the odor of which sent Saranitza and myself to windward. We advised Clisson to fill a few bombs with it, predicting panic to any army so bombarded, but Clisson munched away very coolly, and I retired, motioning my troopers to dismount and eat.

When I was out of the cheese-tainted atmosphere, and out of sight too for that matter, I produced my flask and dried meat and fell to with an appetite.

I sat quite still, the cool hill-winds blowing in my face, musing, eating, drinking, by turns, my hussar's busby and sabre on a rock beside me. In the grass the little ants were already busy with the dropped crumbs; crickets scrambled about, running boldly over my spurred boots, and metallic winged gorse-butterflies flitted and fluttered across my face.

"In the midst of life we are in death," I repeated aloud, watching the ants; a careless movement of my boot heel might have crushed out a dozen lives. I caught a cricket with a quick movement and held it gently between my fingers.

" Poor devil," I said, " what if I should close my hand?"

Then I let it go uninjured, wondering whether God would spare me in battle; and I bit a piece from my sandwich and gazed at my spurs.

I was about to rise, after having taken a last swallow from my flask, and I had already picked up my busby and sabre, when, without the least warning, the bushes beside me parted and a human hand was thrust out. Before I could recover from the shock and seize my revolver, the hand opened, a letter dropped on the grass, and the hand disappeared. In an instant I had leaped into the thicket, crashing and clambering about among the stumps and tangled undergrowth, but, although I could distinctly hear somebody moving farther and farther away, I neither knew in which direction the sound came from nor could I catch a glimpse of a living thing.

At last the sound died away and I listened for a moment and then floundered out of the undergrowth to the open meadow where the letter lay.   Slowly I stooped and picked it up, turning the written side over.   The letter was addressed to me !

I sat down on the grass, casting a nervous glance at the thicket, and tore the letter from its cover.   A sheet of paper, faintly perfumed and covered with long fine writing fluttered out.   This was what I read :

" BELGARDE,
          Thursday Evening.

MY DARLING :
This is my first warning.   The Boznovian army is encamped on the plateau beyond Dragovitza. Push on after them without delay ; they will not stand but will fall back on the Black Fortress of Tchenekoi.   Take the Ravno high-road and halt at Tchatal-Dagh until you hear again from me.   I am with Witch Sylvia and watch her every movement.   I love you ; you must not die.

LINA."

I read the letter three times ; then I stood up, opened my dolman, thrust the letter into my bosom in the general direction of my heart, and walked lightly across the field to where my comrades were lounging.

"Well," said Clisson, " I've finished my cheese.   Your face is scratched; have you been finding some Boznovian peasant girl and have you been conducting yourself with more enthusiasm than discretion?"

"Ah—h! l'amour! l'amour!" sighed the Prince, emptying his bottle of Burgundy and clicking his white teeth together.

"Come along," said I, "I have news for King Casimir."   And I gave the signal to mount.

CHAPTER XV.

THE BATTLE OF DRAGOVITZA.

BEFORE we were fairly in our saddles, the deep crash of a cannon sounded among the trees and rocks, echoing far out across the valley, and I saw a pillar of white smoke drifting from the hill-top where our batteries lay. Again the solemn note of the cannon sounded, and again and yet again, while the hill-top swam in a vast eddy of white clouds through which pale tongues of flame leaped out into the sunshine.

The troop-horses pricked up their soft ears and switched their tails. Far across the valley on the forest-fringed plateau, the shells were falling and exploding in little puffs of smoke, but the masses of infantry had disappeared, probably into the forest, and, through my field-glasses,

I could see the shells drop among the thistles and herbage, bursting in a shower of dirt and shattered shrubs before the intrenchments.

And now the roll of the cannonade increased, roaring, swelling, resounding among the rocks, until it became one deep prolonged peal, and the hill was hidden in billowy clouds.

" Mount !" I cried, " March ! Trot ! Gallop !" and away we clattered in a swirl of dust and leaves.

All the way to headquarters, Clisson and Prince Saranitza and I discussed the meaning of the sudden artillery outburst, and I was wondering how soon we might be expected to move out in force, when a messenger from the King of Caucasia dashed up, ordering Clisson to his regiment, Saranitza to his, and me to report at headquarters.

Half way up the slope we separated, the Prince cantering gaily away to his dragoons, Clisson and my red riders plunging through the maize field toward the hollow, and I, spurring straight up the smoking hill toward the headquarters of King Casimir of Caucasia.

As I guided my horse through the dense cannon mist drifting in from the batteries, the ear-splitting crash of the guns made me dizzy and the sulphurous fog, thickening at every deafening blast, filled my throat and eyes until I could scarcely see or breathe. Half stifled, blinded, and stunned, I finally stumbled up against a vedette and dismounted before the marquee.   In a scarcely audible voice I asked for the King of Caucasia, giving my name to the orderly, and at once I was ushered into the tent where a dozen officers were sitting closely huddled around a small deal table.

" Ha!" said the King of Caucasia when he saw me ; and all the officers turned and regarded me with half-suppressed grins.

" What is this I hear about a bear ?" asked King Casimir angrily.

" Bear ?—your Majesty," I replied, bewildered.

" Yes, a bear," snapped King Casimir,

"it is reported that you found one in the Ezrox station."

" I did," I replied, flushing with annoyance.

" A tame one ? "

"Yes your Majesty."

" Where is it ? "

" In the cavalry ambulance, sire."

" Then read that," said the King, handing me a letter across the table.

" I am to read it ? "

" Yes,—I don't care who reads it, but I 'll be revenged for this insult !" fumed the King.

I read the letter in growing astonishment :

" The Princess Sylvia of Marmora begs to inform King Casimir of Caucasia that she lost her pet bear somewhere on the Ravno highway between the Tiflix notch and Tchatal-Dagh. In case King Casimir should find the bear, will he be kind enough to bring it with him to Belgarde, as the Princess Sylvia would rather have two bears than none at all.

(Signed)   "SYLVIA OF MARMORA."

" There 's a post-script on the other

side," cried the King passionately, and banged his fist on the table.

I turned the sheet of paper and read :

" The bear is called Casimir, but there need be no confusion, for the Princess Sylvia expects to change either the bear's name or the most Christian name of King Casimir when the menagerie arrives."

" Witch Sylvia !" I said, not knowing what else to say.

" The ' menagerie,'" said the King in an awful voice, " means me and the bear. Very good,—very, ve-ry good ! She wants her bear, this Witch Sylvia ;—she shall have her bear. Colonel Steen, you have orders to immediately attach that bear to the personnel of my headquarters, and I will stake my crown that the Princess Sylvia of Marmora receives her property from my own hand."

I saluted, stifling a violent inclination to laugh, and walked out through the smoke again toward the batteries.

The din of the cannon made my ears ache ; I felt the earth tremble beneath me at every explosion. Bugles were sounding too from the masses of crouching infantry, but the shock and pealing crashes from the batteries almost drowned their clangor. As for the drums, not a tap could be heard although the troops seemed to read the signal from the vibrating drum-sticks; for now long lines of infantry rose up from thicket and meadow-grass, and started off down the hillside in open order. For a while I could see their flags moving, well ahead of the line of battle, and farther on, the skirmish lines, hurrying out through the veil of smoke, while above their heads red jets of flame leaped and played and lashed out through the cannon gloom, licking the edges of the sulphurous cloud with a hundred dazzling tongues.

Taxil and Babu passed and I called to them, but they could not hear me of course, and I followed them and laid my hand on Taxil's arm.

"What the devil are they doing anyway?" I shouted close to his ear.

"You need n't howl that way," said the Duke much amused, "you need only lower your voice to be understood.   Vladina's division is moving on the plateau under cover of the cannonade," he added.

I thought of my letter and Lina's advice and decided, as the troops were doing what Lina had said they should do, that there was no immediate need of making King Casimir my confidant.

" The cannonade will slacken in a few minutes," observed Babu, rolling a bit of Ispha nut under his tongue, " as soon as Vladina's troops get to the foot of the plateau."

" Where 's that bear ? " I asked abruptly.

" In the ambulance," replied Taxil.

" Send the brute to King Casimir at once then," I said, and left them, returning their astonished salutes impatiently.

" Sure as guns," said I to myself, "the cavalry will be needed as soon as Vladina's infantry get onto the plateau " ; and I walked up to my horse, mounted, and picked my way through a mass of artillery and baggage trains to the hollow below the hill where my own regiment lay.

The troopers were still lolling about on

17

the ground beside the stream and the horses cropped the grass or tore strips of tender bark and clusters of leaves from the bushes ; but I saw that Clisson and Bombwitz were mounted and were attentively examining the valley through their binoculars.

The cannonade had already begun to slacken as I rode up to them ; and I was able to make myself heard without danger of throat rupture.

"Aha !" cried Clisson briskly, " if I am not mistaken, Count Vladina is moving on the plateau."

" You 're right," said I, " and I suppose we will be wanted presently. I see that Prince Saranitza's dragoons are already in position. What a hasty young man he is ! "

" The cannon have ceased," observed Bombwitz, "and here comes an aid-de-camp with orders."

" Where 's my trumpeter ? " I cried ; "here ! sound boots-and-saddles ! Clisson, does his Majesty go with us ? Yes ? Good then ; — General Bombwitz, pray find the King, for these orders admit of

no delay. Sound the 'Salute to the King!'
Ah, here comes his Majesty with Taxil
and Babu.   Clisson, I lead, remember,—
your horse's nose is not to pass my holster unless I 'm hit.   Sound and mount!
March!   Trot!"

The grassy meadow shook as we moved
out of the hollow and down the slope into
the plain.   Out of the corner of my eye
I saw Saranitza's dragoons trotting abreast
of us and beyond them other lines of cavalry, all moving at a trot over the vast
plain toward the plateau at the end of the
valley.

"The Duke of Etropolis commands in
person," said Clisson at my elbow; "he
is over there with the Curtina division
and the Bazoum lancers."

"He does n't command this regiment,"
I said flippantly; "we will beat him up
the hill!"

"Go easy, all the same," said Clisson
laughing and bringing his horse a pace
closer.

"Stop that, Clisson," I said; "I am
leading this charge."   Then I bared my

sabre and raised it in the sunlight, half turning in my saddle.

"Draw sabres! Gallop!" I shouted, and the trumpets pealed a stirring response.

"You'd better let me give the orders," suggested Clisson, coming closer again.

"There's only one more to give," said I, "and I'll give it when the time comes."

Nearer and nearer we drew to the foot of the grey plateau where already Vladina's endless columns were hurrying up the slope, flags tossing, bayonets flashing in the sun.

"They'll get there first!" I panted to Clisson.

"Of course," he said, "that's what was planned!"

"I don't care a damn what was planned!" I cried,—for I was feverishly excited with the clash of arms and the splendid sweeping gallop,—"I'm going to get there first!"

"Wait!" urged Clisson, but my answer was to rise in my stirrups and swing my sabre.

"Charge!" I shouted, and the trumpets answered swiftly, and the Hussars of the Body-Guard plunged forward cheering, breasting the slope like a tempest crested wave, dashing up, onto, and over the shell-torn summit, and on across the plateau.

Right in front of us lay a low line of breastworks from the embrasures and angles of which protruded cannon.

"It's too late to halt!" gasped Clisson; "charge the batteries, in God's name!"

"Charge!" I shouted, and "Charge!" burst from the silvery bugles, and away we dashed, sabres swinging in the sunshine.

My eyes were fixed on the black muzzles of the cannon, and I vaguely wondered when the storm would burst upon us, but I was not nervous for I felt the grand stride of my horse and the intoxication of my first charge, and my ears were filled with the clamor of a thousand voices, thrilling me like the roaring of a mighty wind :

"For the King! Charge! For the King!"

"Now!" bellowed Clisson, "over the earth-works! In we go!" and the horses hurled themselves furiously upon the in-. trenchments,—and lo! we were inside.

At first, in the confusion and shouting and neighing of horses, I could not comprehend exactly why we were not engaged in a terrible hand to hand struggle, but gradually, as I mastered my horse and turned my blood-shot eyes, I saw no signs of any enemy, only the plunging, prancing, vociferous squadrons of my own regiment; and now also, the first columns of Vladina's infantry appearing over the hill-crest, and Prince Saranitza's dragoons sweeping in from the other side.

"What does it all mean?" I stammered, looking helplessly at Clisson who sat on his dripping horse, smiling grimly.

"Oh nothing," he said, "nothing,— nothing except that we charged empty intrenchments and dummy cannon,—which," he added with a roar of laughter, "our artillery has been shelling for three hours!"

"Dummy cannon!" I repeated incredulous and angry.

"Look for yourself," said Clisson.

It was too true. Painted logs lay in the emplacements, some not even mounted on wheels. The flag, flying from the breastworks was merely a peasant woman's red and white apron, and a hundred or two battered old helmets, stuck upon sticks completed the miserable farce.

"Good heavens!" I muttered, "this is terrible, Clisson!"

"Oh, not so bad," he said, choking with laughter, "you know we took a prisoner yesterday—"

I wheeled my horse abruptly and rode out of ear-shot; and the things I said must have turned the angels pale.

A trooper trotted up to me grinning and saluting. He held the captured flag, the peasant woman's apron, in his hand.

"Throw that rag away!" I said sulkily.

"There is something written on it, mon Colonel," said the trooper doubtfully, and held the apron spread toward me. On it was painted in black letters:

"Compliments of the Princess Sylvia of Marmora."

My teeth chattered with rage and I felt my face grow hot and cold alternately. At last I controlled myself and found my voice.

"Take the captured standard to King Casimir of Caucasia," I said, and went away to hide my mortification and nurse my wrath against this devil in woman's shape who had twice made me ridiculous before my regiment.

CHAPTER XVI.

AN UNEXPECTED JOURNEY.

THE army camped that night on the plateau. Vladina's division of infantry occupied the intrenchments, the artillery was parked in the rear, and the cavalry, except the Bazoum lancers, held the plateau, from the earthworks to the forest, the vedettes of their advanced posts patrolling the Ravno high-road to within hailing distance of the walls of Tchatal-Dagh. The Bazoum lancers guarded the train-des-equipages, and incidentally, the telephone wires to the Ezrox Station.

On receipt of the captured apron with the insulting inscription, the King of Caucasia had sent for me. I found him in a towering rage, but I was in no mood to be trifled with and I gave him to understand so at once. It relieved him somewhat to see that I was fully as angry as he was, for he imagined, I fancy, that the whole army was laughing at him. As I, rightly or wrongly, imagined the same thing concerning myself, we soon came to an understanding that boded ill for this low-comedy Princess. In a paroxysm of confidence I told the King about my means of communication through Lina, and showed him all that was necessary of her letter. It seemed to impress him considerably, for in spite of his outburst, I noticed that the mention of Witch Sylvia was received with something that bordered on uneasiness.

"She's a devil, that's what she is," said the King, "and it won't do to ignore her in this campaign. If it were only her brother whom we had to deal with I'd march on Belgarde to-night."

"We will be in Tchatal-Dagh by sunrise anyway," I observed.

The King turned and looked at Daniel, the bear, who lay quietly sleeping under a shelter tent at the door of the marquee. I saw the King's face grow red again as he remembered the insult to his Christian name.

"Pray forget it, your Majesty," I said, "we will pack this Marmora figurante back to her own country before the end of the week."

The King nodded and buried his nose in his hands. He did look like the bear, —a little.

The Duke of Etropolis followed by Saranitza, Vladina, and General Brimborio came in and the King told them about my secret communication with the palace at Belgarde.

"Probably I shall receive another note after we enter Tchatal-Dagh," said I, "and in that case I will bring it at once to your Majesty."

"I hope it may give us some idea of the Black Fortress," observed Vladina, "I don't like the looks of it particularly."

"We must storm it," said Prince Saranitza with a careless smile at me.

"What we need will be siege guns, and we'll have to sit down before Belgarde and wait for them as the Germans had to wait before the walls of Paris," muttered the Duke of Etropolis.

"But we can't wait," said the King, "we've got to get into Belgarde before Russia begins to move."

"Pooh?" said Prince Saranitza, "Russia!"   And he snapped his fingers.

"We'd be in a beautiful predicament if you had your way," said Count Vladina laughing and patting Saranitza on the arm.

"Perhaps," said the King, looking at me, "you will have something to tell us by morning."

"I trust so," I replied fervently. "My regiment is restless and anxious to come to close quarters, but what can we do if the Boznovians play circus tricks on us and run?"

"It is most mortifying to me," said the Duke of Etropolis ; "here we have marched for miles through an admittedly hostile country, we have driven in the enemy's out-posts, we have occupied villages, we have bombarded a fortified plateau for hours, and finally, we have hurled our whole army against it.   The result is that not one drop of blood has been spilled, not one prisoner taken."

"Pardon," said Saranitza, "the bear—"

I rose, deeply offended, and begged the King's permission to withdraw.

"It was an ill-timed pleasantry, Prince Saranitza," said the King; and the Prince jumped up and came frankly to me to ask my pardon. I granted it heartily, for I was becoming very fond of the hare-brained dragoon, and I pressed his proffered hand warmly, ignoring the twinkle in his eyes.

At the same moment King Theobold of Boznovia entered the tent, followed by their Graces of Taxil and Babu.

"The cavalry have scoured the forest for miles," said King Theobald, returning the greetings of the company; "Colonel Clisson says that he'll stake his head that there is not a Boznovian soldier in this section of the country."

"Then where the mischief did the troops go—the infantry that occupied the plateau before we opened on them?" demanded the Duke of Etropolis.

"Our advanced posts report that a heavy column of the enemy passed through Tchatal-Dagh, retreating toward Belgarde," said Taxil, who had just been visiting the pickets and whose uniform was yellow with dust.

"Well," said Saranitza resignedly, "if this is the sort of thing they are going to keep up, I don't see much fun ahead unless we take the Black Fortress by assault—"

"Be quiet," said King Casimir, "you don't know what you 're saying. Fortresses of the first class are not knocked over like card houses."

Saranitza bowed good humoredly and looked askance at the bear.

Babu chewed an Ispha nut and stared at the company with his great round eyes.

"Well gentlemen," began King Casimir, rising, when a sudden commotion at the door of the tent arrested his attention. An officer and two troopers appeared, leading a man dressed in the costume of a Boznovian peasant. The troopers were hussars, the officer was Clisson.

"At last," said Saranitza, "we 've taken a prisoner I do believe!"

I had to laugh, but the King of Caucasia stepped forward frowning and motioning Clisson to bring the fellow in.

"We caught him, your Majesty, in the woods, trying to steal past our vedettes," said Clisson.

"I am no spy," said the man coolly, "and I can prove it."

"Prove it," said the King.

"I will, if any gentleman will conduct me to Colonel Steen of the Hussar-Guard."

"Oho!" said the King of Caucasia, "perhaps you bring Colonel Steen certain information."

The man, a bearded young peasant, shut his lips tightly and looked at the King.

"Speak," cried King Casimir.

"Then bring me to Colonel Steen," replied the peasant doggedly. The King nodded to me and I stepped forward confronting the fellow.

He surveyed me from head to foot without speaking.

"Well," said I, "I am Colonel Steen of the Hussar-Guard."

"How am I to know," he asked.

"On the word of a King," said King Theobald of Boznovia haughtily.

The man glanced at the King and then at me.

"Come," said I, "have you a message for me?"

Then he came close to me and whispered in my ear; "from whom do you expect a message?"

"From my promised wife," I said simply.

"Her name?"

"I do not know it; I call her Lina."

"Good," said the man smiling, and dropping his mask of caution, "now listen and then tell these very noble officers whether or not I am a spy. Your promised wife who is a domestic in the service of the Princess Sylvia of Marmora bids you know that my message is genuine because of the token she gave to you in the Tiflix valley," and he pointed to the golden image of Sainte-Catharine glistening on my tunic.

I turned to the company and said aloud : "This man is no spy; listen to what he has to say." Then I told him to speak up before all the people present ; and he did so.

"I am sent here," he said, "to tell you that the Boznovian forces are in full retreat and have this night re-entered Belgarde. The Black Fortress of Tchenekoi is not heavily garrisoned, but there are mines and torpedoes and the heaviest guns north of Italy, all of which will cause you months of delay unless you can avoid them. As the Black Fortress of Tchenekoi is the key to Belgarde, it is necessary to find some one who understands how to unlock the door. This can be done. The person who sends me here and who is known to Colonel Steen, offers to show you herself how it is possible to safely enter the Black Fortress."

18

The King of Caucasia nodded approval and motioned the messenger to proceed.

"Your Majesty," he said, "this secret was not entrusted to me.   It is only from this person's lips that you may be informed.   Therefore she who sends me wishes to meet you to-night at eleven. Tchatal-Dagh is not occupied at present by the Boznovian army, and the rendezvous designated is the Lion fountain in the public square.   I will be there to recognize you and guide you.   You must come secretly and without heavy escort, otherwise the alarm would spread, the Boznovian army might envelope the town, and the last chance to learn the way safely into the Black Fortress would be lost."

The King looked at the fellow suspiciously for a moment; then, turning to me ; "Do you vouch for this man ?"

"I do," I said.

"And I also," said King Theobald, "if Colonel Steen does."

I thanked King Theobald and turned to the messenger again.

"Am I to go?" I asked.

"The secret of the Black Fortress will not be disclosed except to the King of Caucasia and to yourself, and to those whom you select to accompany you," said the man.

"Then I select you," said King Casimir looking at the King of Boznovia.

The implied distrust sent a faint color into King Theobald's cheeks, but he drew himself up and thanked the King of Caucasia for his courtesy. There was much of nobility in his carriage and face and I think it shamed King Casimir for he hastily designated Prince Saranitza and their Graces of Taxil and Babu as his escort, and then withdrew to consult the Duke of Etropolis.

"At eleven," I said to the messenger, giving him all the money I had about me ; and I dismissed him, telling Clisson to escort him as far as the walls of Tchatal-Dagh.

Generals Bombwitz and Brimborio, and Count Vladina joined with the Duke of Etropolis in trying to dissuade us from going, but, when I told them enough of the case to make them easier, they agreed that it was a rare opportunity and was in fact a miracle of good fortune. So we sat chatting and discussing the campaign and the chances of being in Belgarde by dinner time to-morrow : and we were all very merry over our mess, drinking to each other and to the two kingdoms ; and also we drank confusion to the Russian puppet, who, with his sister, Witch Sylvia, "tyrannized" over the Boznovian people.

One by one the regimental officers rose and left ; the two puffy Generals and the keen-eyed Duke of Etropolis being the last to retire, and, about half past ten o'clock, the two Monarchs, Taxil, Babu, Saranitza, and I, called for our horses.

It was a clear star-lit evening when we left the intrenchments, escorted by a peloton of lancers, and trotted away down the Ravno road toward Tchatal-Dagh ; but, before we had passed our extreme outposts, the sky suddenly became covered with spotted fleecy clouds, stretching in layers and strata from horizon to horizon.

As we entered the causeway that leads through the dismantled crumbling walls of Tchatal-Dagh, the stars had all disappeared and the darkness around us was only lighted by a few wretched lanterns swinging from the straggling houses along the street.

Our lancers, who had galloped on ahead, now returned to say that the town was deserted, save by a cowering peasant or two; so we rode on, I leading, until we came to a long dark alley through which we could see a lantern burning above the Lion fountain in the square. One or two terrified towns-people came to their doors at the sound of the horses' hoofs, but, at such doors, we stationed a lancer, with orders to prevent egress until we returned. The two Kings rode together, then followed their Graces of Taxil and Babu, and after them, much against his will, trotted Prince Saranitza. I led the cavalcade, and posted the last lancer of the escort, just as we came in sight of the Lion fountain.

"There is somebody waiting there

under that lantern," said King Casimir,
"do you see?"

"I see," I answered, "it is our guide;"
and I rode up to him and hailed him in a
low voice.

Without a word he turned and walked
swiftly across the square toward a house
that stood alone in a garden, a little back
from the street. We followed, and at a
motion from our guide, we dismounted at
the gate and entered the garden single
file, leading our horses around to the rear
of the house. Here I saw that the house
faced also on another street, completely
cut off from the square except by the
footpath through the garden.

"Leave your horses with me," said the
peasant; "go straight to the door and
open it, Colonel Steen."

I felt my way carefully through the
shrubbery and up the path to the door.
The door opened before I could touch it
and a lighted lantern swung in my face.

Dazzled for an instant, I recoiled, but
a voice that I knew called to me to enter,
and I sprang in and bent my lips to the

most beautiful hand in the world.   Then I gazed earnestly, rapturously, at the hooded face before me, repeating, " Lina, Lina," while the two Kings and the others entered without ceremony and stood watching me.

" Come," said Lina taking my hand in hers, and we stepped into a square room to the left, where some candles were burning brightly on a table.

For a moment, as the others brushed past us into the room, we stood close together, hand in hand.   With a sudden movement of tenderness she bent and touched the gold Sainte-Catharine on my breast, then, gently disengaging her hand, she drew me back into the shadow of the hall-way, put both arms about my neck, and raised her face to mine.

Then a terrible thing occurred.   Out of the shadowy corners on every side sprang scores of soldiers ; there came a startled cry, a crash, a brief struggle from the room where the Kings had entered ; I heard Saranitza shout and I heard his cry of defiance smothered as by a hand over his mouth.   And all the time I was twisting and turning and struggling to free my body from the close embrace of the girl I loved, but her young limbs wound about mine like steel encased in velvet, and in another instant a man seized me from behind, binding ankles and elbows with incredible swiftness.

And, as the light of the lantern fell squarely on his face, I saw it was my peasant messenger,—bereft of beard and moustache,—and a sudden recollection blazed up within me ;—ah !—I knew him now, that black-eyed Russian who had dismounted at my door in the Tiflix valley, and who accepted a glass of wine from me before he and his comrade rode away on their bicycles !   And Lina ! There she stood, looking straight into my face from beneath the shadow of her hood ; and I opened my mouth and cursed her treachery which had cost me more than my life, more than my love,—my honour.

One by one the Boznovian soldiers led their prisoners from the room beyond, —the King of Caucasia,▪ the King of

Boznovia, and the two Dukes.   Saranitza
had been knocked senseless in the struggle, and they carried him out between
four soldiers.

I heard Lina ask where the droschskys
were, and at the same moment the sound
of wheels from the back street came distinctly to my ears. Two soldiers picked me
up from the floor and carried me, strapped
like a pappoose, down through the garden
to the street.   A droschsky was waiting ;
Lina sprang in, I was placed beside her,
and, at a signal from the Russian, the
vehicle started away at a furious pace.

"Lina," said I at last, "you are a spy
and you have done your duty by your
Princess and your country.   I do not
speak of what my love has been for you,
—more than life itself to me, but now,
that you have done your duty and I have
lost my honour, I beg you to let me die
before the rifles of ten Boznovian soldiers ; for never again can I look the
King, or any man in the face."

"The Princess will decide," she said in
a strained voice.

"That devil, Witch Sylvia!" I cried fiercely.

"The Princess Sylvia of Marmora!" said Lina with cold deliberation.

Then I answered very humbly, "God keep my soul from meeting yours for all time to come." And, as we sped on through the night, I closed my eyes and prayed that my life might be taken quickly, for my torture was more than I could bear.

CHAPTER XVII.

THE BLACK FORTRESS.

THE cold white morning light fell in a pallid bar across my bed as I sat up, bewildered, rubbing my hot eyes. Then, as I looked from the iron-grilled windows to the stone floor, I understood, and I dropped back upon the bed. One by one the events of the night came back to me, the touch of those soft hands, the kiss,—then the foul treachery, the clang of arms and the struggle,—ah ! now I remembered the swift journey, the lurching of the droschsky and the galloping horses ; I remembered the sudden trample of an unseen escort, the crack of the long lashed whip as we clattered into a stony street and whirled on and on, the shrill challenges of sentinels ringing in my ears. Could I doubt where they were taking me ? " Pass !" cried a Boznovian sentry, and "Pass !" echoed the guards from rampart and bastion, and we dashed on through the night while the sombre walls seemed to fly past, and tower and battlement swam in a grey haze against the paling sky. Silent, motionless, Lina crouched beside me, never by word or gesture betraying consciousness of my presence until the first lantern swung from the fortifications and the last Boznovian soldier greeted us with a deep hail. Then she suddenly sat up and I heard her thank God, and every word cut me like a knife-thrust. Again, after we had passed through a long stony court, faced by dim walls, she stooped and flung her mantle across me to shield me from the damp. But I thrust it fiercely aside with my bound wrists. For a moment she looked at me, seeming to hesitate, then she whipped out a slender blade, swiftly severed the rope that held my wrists and ankles, and slowly returned the jewelled-hilted knife to her girdle.

"Give me the knife," I said at last,

"I shall never again ask anything from you."

"Hush," she said in that strange voice that I had never before heard.

I listened to the gallop of the escort; the vehicle lurched and shook. I leaned over and peered into the twilight of the morning. On every side pressed the Boznovian cavalry, grey with dust, sabres shining in the pallor of the coming dawn.

"Give me the knife," I repeated, "it is as honourable a death as to die like Major Panitza. Give me the knife, or I will throw myself under the hoofs of the escort!"

"Hush, you don't know what you say," she said again, and at the same moment a heavy voice cried "Halt!" and the droschsky drew up before a massive wall barred with iron.

One by one the other vehicles drove by and I saw my comrades dismount and pass before me, heavily guarded. Last of all came Prince Saranitza, borne by four soldiers, but whether he was stunned or whether he was dead I did not know.

Then a cavalryman touched me on the arm and bade me follow him. Lina had disappeared.

And now I was lying here on my iron bed, the white dawn creeping in through the barred slit in the wall, my heart numb with the agony of grief and shame.

Across the room—it was too vast to call it a cell—lay Prince Saranitza on his bed of iron, sleeping peacefully. Ah! but when he should awake what words would he have for me—what words would he find to express his horror and scorn of what he must believe to be my treachery? I raised my head and looked at him with feverish eyes, holding my breath, for I dreaded the awakening. He lay there quite peacefully, his blond clipped curls on his arm, one hand half opened on his breast. He was so young, so boyish—I could not believe that his fate was to die before a firing platoon with twelve bullets in his breast. Then I remembered that picture I had seen in *Harper's Weekly*, the death of Panitza.

And so, after all, I also was going to

die with my back to a stone wall. My breath came faster and a sickly chill ran through me. And yet, if death might only come before Saranitza awoke to turn his scornful eyes on me and call me traitor,—if they would shoot me quickly so that at last it would be over and I should have some rest from the shame and the gnawing misery in my breast,— then, ah then, I would have welcomed it, and I believe that I could have faced the rifles with a lighter heart than I had ever faced the woman I loved.

In those miserable moments as I lay there, watching Saranitza's placid breathing, I thought too of Marjory Grey, and I realized then that I no longer loved her, for, if I had, I should have known it in that moment.

I was, as yet, not able to understand that I had lost Lina forever,—that the woman I had loved had proved to be the lowest of human creatures. I only knew that there was a great sorrow bowing me to the ground with its weight, that all that made life worth living was gone, and that I longed for the rest that only death could bring.

Suddenly Prince Saranitza moved in his slumber, opened his eyes, and hastily sat up, throwing the covers from his body.

"Hello!" he cried, catching sight of me, "what the deuce is all this, Steen?"

"Don't you remember?" I stammered.

"Remember? Ah—um—yes, let me see—oh!"

I saw that he recollected the sudden surprise in the house in Tchatal-Dagh.

"We were ambushed and captured," I said.

He nodded, rubbing his head with his hand. Then looking at me he said: "There was treachery, was there not?"

"There was," I replied, "the woman who sent me the message was a spy in the Boznovian service, and the man who brought it and met us at the Lion fountain in Tchatal-Dagh was a Russian secret agent."

"Oh," said the Prince rather blankly,

—" I believe I was knocked on the head, was I not ? "

" Yes," I said.

There was a break in my voice—the strain was severe,—and the Prince noticed it. He looked at me curiously, then a change came over his face, and he sprang up and walked straight up to me.

" See here, old fellow," he said, laying his arm lightly on my shoulder, " don't think for one instant that I suspect you. Heaven knows your face tells your story plainly enough for all the world to read."

It was so sudden, so unexpected, that it completely upset me. I dropped my face in my hands and the tears dripped through my fingers to the floor.

" Damn it all !" said the Prince, quite as much upset as I was,—" you did n't think that we would imagine anything to your discredit, did you ? Come, buck up, old fellow ! Why, I 'd trust you with the woman I love, as far as your honour is concerned,—but," he added, trying to laugh, " not as far as your military knowledge is concerned."

19

I raised my head and looked at him, smiling, and brushing my eyes on my sleeve.

"You 're no diplomat," he said, "now are you?"

"I 'm nothing of any consequence," I replied, "I 'm no soldier,—I 'm simply an every-day fool."

"Nonsense," said Saranitza, pulling on his spurred boots and walking over to the iron wash-basin ; "you did your best, as we all did.   We were simply outwitted and here we are.   I suppose the two Kings and the Dukes were taken?"

"Yes," I said sadly, "what can they be thinking of me?"

"They 'll think as I do or I 'll know the reason why," blurted out the Prince.

"I 'm afraid we none of us will have very long to think on this earth," I said sadly.

The Prince looked around at me, the water streaming from hair and face.

"You think they will shoot us?" he asked.

"I suppose there is little doubt of

King Theobald's fate and the fate reserved for Taxil and Babu and myself," I answered. "I don't see, however, why they should not treat you and King Casimir in a civilized manner. You are not Boznovians who have risen in revolt."

"I'm not a Caucasian either," said Prince Saranitza, "I'm an Austrian and stand the same chance that you, who are an American, do."

"But," I said curiously, "I thought you were a Caucasian Prince,—you hold a commission in the Caucasian army."

"Just for fun, that's all. I lived in Vienna but I resigned a lieutenancy in the Guards to accept a colonelcy in the Caucasian army. As soon as I was made general,—and the King promised me my epaulettes for next New Year's,—I was going back to Austria to marry on a decent salary."

I looked at the young fellow in deep pity.

"Yes, that's why I left Vienna. I wanted to be able to support a wife as you Americans look at it. I could have married last year had I chosen to stand in the position of a poor Prince marrying a rich American girl."

"An American!" I cried.

"Yes," he said laughing, "and perhaps that's the reason I have taken so to you."

He came toward me, rubbing his head with the coarse prison towel.

"I wonder whether you know her," he said; "I met her at a ball given in Paris last winter. It was simply to see her to yield to the enchantment of her beauty. I hardly dared ask to be presented;—I can scarcely realize yet that she has promised to wait for me."

"You will see her again," I said in a low voice; "a regular officer, Austrian or Caucasian, will certainly be treated as a prisoner of war and not as a revolutionist."

"Qui sait?" said the Prince soberly.

We found soap and towels enough to satisfy anybody and an abundance of cold water in the iron sink. The Prince had a pocket comb and we succeeded in arranging each other's hair, for there was no mirror in the room.

It was eight o'clock in the morning by my watch when a soldier appeared and told us to follow him. We passed out of the massive door-way and entered a long dimly lighted passage. At the end of this passage we found a room, comfortably upholstered, in the middle of which stood a breakfast table with seats arranged for six people. Military servants stood silently behind each chair, and, as we entered, from an opposite door emerged the King of Caucasia, and the Ex-King of Boznovia, followed by their anxious Graces of Taxil and Babu.

When the King of Caucasia saw me he frowned and whispered something to King Theobald, but the latter smiled and shook his head, greeting me at the same time very cordially.

When the two Monarchs were seated, we took our places as designated by the King of Caucasia.

The breakfast was well cooked and well served, but I could not eat and did not even pretend to try until Saranitza urged me. Both King Theobald and Prince

Saranitza were very kind, saying every-thing possible to put me at my ease, and at last I could see that even the King of Caucasia no longer believed me guilty of the horrible treachery that had made us all prisoners of the new Boznovian King and his crafty sister, the Princess Sylvia.

As for Taxil and Babu, they were very mournful, for they suspected what their fate was to be; still they managed to eat a fair breakfast, especially Babu, whose inordinate use of the Ispha nut gave him an appetite that not even the fear of ap-proaching dissolution could dull or dis-courage.   Taxil also bore up more bravely than I might have suspected, and I do believe that grief for his exploded railroad scheme had as much to do with his un-happiness as did the suspicion of impend-ing execution.

King Theobald bore himself like a true King, cheerfully and gallantly.   He thanked us all for having aided him and said that he alone was responsible for the revolution.   He neither blamed me for having counselled him badly nor did he even refer to his miserable aunt, the Dowager Duchess von Schwiggle who, after all, was the root of the whole evil.

This comforted me greatly for it seemed easier to die for a gallant monarch than to be shot to death on account of a royal buffoon.

King Casimir said little, and what he did say was not in the choicest of language, for he could not forget that he had been outwitted by a woman, and he took it hard.

"I should think," observed Saranitza, "that your Majesty would consider it an honour to be conquered by so beautiful a princess as the Princess Sylvia of Marmora is said to be."

"The devil fly away with the Princess Sylvia of Marmora," cried King Casimir.

At a sign from King Theobald the military servants withdrew, leaving us alone in the great comfortable room.

"I suppose we are in that cursed Black Fortress," observed King Casimir grimly.

"I suppose so,—the Black Fortress of Tchenekoi," replied Prince Saranitza with a careless glance around the room, "I wonder what our army will do?"

We all sat silently staring at the table.

"It will take them some time to get siege guns in position," ventured Taxil.

"Time enough for these Boznovians to play the mischief with us," said King Casimir.   "The game's up, that's certain, for Russia won't stand this row,—no, not another week."

"It's been a very bloodless war," observed Saranitza ; "I'm not aware of any damage done except a crack I got on the head last night."

"The whole thing is ridiculous !" fumed King Casimir, "we shall be the laughing stock of Europe for this campaign ! And all on account of Witch Sylvia ! Oh, it makes me hot and cold when I think of it—"

A door was suddenly flung open and a tall wiry young man in the uniform of the Boznovian Life-Guards appeared.   For a second he paused on the threshold, then walked swiftly toward the table and sat down, facing us.   The door at the end of the room swung to with a crash and the echoes struck sharply in the silent room.

"I am the King of Boznovia," he said abruptly, "and I have come here in behalf of my sister, the Princess Sylvia of Marmora, to announce to you the judgment passed last night."

He stood up, looked at King Theobald, took a dozen nervous strides up and down the room, and came back.

"The judgment pronounced by the court-martial is death!" he said; "and I, Rupert of Boznovia, approve!"

King Theobald passed his hand over his forehead slowly.

"We are to be executed?" he asked gravely.

"I did not say so," said Rupert of Boznovia casting a keen glance at me; "I said that the court-martial has pronounced the death sentence."

Then he sat down again, his silver cuirass ringing, his sabre clashing softly on the eastern rugs that covered the stone floor.

A minute of perfect silence ensued.

Taxil drank a glass of water mechanically and Saranitza twisted his blond moustache.

"Listen!" said Rupert of Boznovia, fixing his grey eyes on King Theobald, "the court has condemned you to be shot to-morrow at sunrise in the presence of the garrison of this fortress and of the city of Belgarde. It is a just verdict!—I say it is a just verdict!" he repeated with a passionate gesture. "Is his Grace of Taxil better than Major Panitza who was shot for less? Is his Grace of Babu less culpable? And you, Theobald of Taximbourg, driven from this capital of Belgarde by your own people, are you, who return at the head of a Caucasian army to ravage with fire and sword,—are you less guilty than was Stambouloff? What treason is this that I, Rupert of Boznovia and Marmora, should endure it? Am I to submit to invasion and insult? My trust is held by grace of God and the Czar; and the Boznovian people have put their trust in me!" He sprang from his chair again and paced the room restlessly. I saw the King's mouth tighten under his beard

and I saw Prince Saranitza, cool and un-
ruffled, twisting his blond moustache.

King Rupert of Boznovia was still
pacing the room, his white-gloved hands
clasped behind him, his silver sabre bang-
ing at every stride.   Presently he turned
sharply in his tracks and made a menacing
gesture toward us.

"You who come to drive me out," he
cried, "you who come with hired armies,
—troops to whom you promise the sack-
ing of my city of Belgarde—"

"Pardon," said King Theobald quietly,
"you have been misinformed."

"Did you not promise it!" cried Rupert angrily.

"No," said King Theobald.

There was something in his tone that
comforted us all I think,—us who were
about to die for his cause.

King Rupert came nearer.

"What was the price then?" he demanded harshly.

King Theobald turned to the King of
Caucasia.

"Am I at liberty to satisfy this young

man ?" he asked coolly.   King Casimir nodded.   There was an evil gleam in his eyes.   Then Theobald of Taximbourg stood up and faced the young King of Boznovia.

"I will answer your question," he said pleasantly, "I promised that Caucasia should have free passage for her ships into the Balkan Sea.   And now I wish to say a little more.   I alone am to blame, —I alone am guilty and worthy of the penalty that your honourable court has fixed upon.   It was I who stirred up the revolt, it was I who persuaded the Duke of Taxil and the Duke of Babu to join me.   I alone sought out his Majesty King Casimir and I persuaded him and his officers.   That I have been a bad King, and an incompetent one, that I have cared nothing for power, or for the country of Boznovia, that I have been weak and incapable, is not for me to confess to you but to God—before I die. Your honourable court-martial has decided and I doubt not that the people of Boznovia will uphold you and applaud the sentence.   Then

let it be carried out,—but on me alone,
for these gentlemen who so gallantly cast
their fortunes with me do not deserve
death, and you will find, Rupert of Mar-
.mora, that they will serve Boznovia,
under you as faithfully as they would
have served her under me. I ask. that
the sentence of the court be carried out
on me at once."

In an instant we were all on our feet,
crying out, gesticulating, crowding before
King Theobald.

"Listen, King Rupert," I shouted in
the babel of voices, "I was chief con-
spirator, I drove his Majesty to this war,
I alone am to blame."

"Who are you?" said Rupert haughtily,—"an American?"

"I am that American who set a hundred thousand men marching on your city
of Belgarde!" I cried, meeting his glance
with a glance as steady and proud.

"Silence!" cried Saranitza, "if his
Majesty, King Theobald is to die, we who
fought for him demand a place by his
side!"

"The King is not to die!" I said loudly, "I am the root of this conspiracy and when the root is killed what need to fear? If Russia will allow King Theobald to live in peace in his own country. of Taximbourg, he will never think of Boznovia again."

As we stood, pressing before Rupert of Boznovia, the light from the barred windows streaming over our faces and brilliant uniforms, somewhere far on the bastions a great gun crashed and the deep echoes reverberated through the prison.

"Do you hear?" cried Rupert furiously," "that cannon-shot means that your army is before Belgarde! Shame on you, Theobald of Taximbourg!—and shame on you, Casimir of Caucasia!—you who bring death and destruction to a peaceful nation! I tell you that your sentence is just and I, Rupert of Bosnovia, approve."

He drew himself up, very pale. I saw my own face, distorted, reflected in his polished cuirass. Then his voice changed:

he touched the hilt of his sabre in a hesitating manner looking from one to the other of us.

"The sentence of the court-martial will not stand," he said at last, "because of my sister's wish. Her Royal Highness, the Princess Sylvia of Marmora, has decided that your fate shall lie with yourselves. I do not seek for vengeance : vengeance is beneath me. As for justice— God alone may deal it out—I dare not attempt it. What I have a right to demand is the safety of my people and the safety of my family and myself. And to that end, I, deferring to the wish of my sister the Princess Sylvia, do hereby offer to you your freedom on these conditions."

He paused, looking from one to the other, fingering his twisted sabre hilt. Then he went on :

"Casimir of Caucasia, go to your troops and lead them back to Bazoum. And that you may not stand ashamed in the face of all Christendom I will concede to you the free passage into the Balkan Sea. If you have any officer here attached to your person or your army, take him with you,—go, and let us live in peace."

He turned to King Theobald :

"Give me your word as a man that never again will you by force seek to re-enter Bosnovia, then go in peace to your own country of Taximbourg where neither Czar nor King shall ever trouble you. My sister, the Princess Sylvia, will pledge her word for yours ; and the Czar listens when she speaks. Take with you the Duke of Taxil and the Duke of Babu. I freely grant the Duke of Taxil his railway from his mines to my capital of Belgarde. It will be good for all concerned."

Then King Theobald stepped forward and thanked King Rupert very simply, and the King of Caucasia, pale with joy at the thought that his two torpedo boats might cruize about the Balkan Sea, stammered his thanks, and Taxil, overjoyed, wept a little and swore that, mines or no mines, he would never enter Boznovia again but would cheerfully cultivate maize and vineyards and domestic virtues in the

Duchy of Taxil for the rest of his life. Babu said nothing but he looked very grateful and chewed an Ispha nut.

"Hark!" cried Rupert as another heavy explosion shook the room and set the glassware tinkling on the table, "that is the second gun and your army has advanced to the extreme limits of Tchatal-Dagh. Go and withdraw your troops; let us live peacefully, King Casimir, and remember that my ports and cities are open to your trade. Theobald of Taximbourg, I send you a suitable escort as I do for King Casimir."

With a sudden gesture, not unfriendly, and entirely courteous, Rupert of Boznovia turned and passed swiftly out by the door through which he had entered. A moment later an escort of Boznovian Life-Guards tramped into the room and halted, sabres at salute, helmets and cuirasses glittering like mirrors.

One by one we passed out between the motionless lines, touching our caps in salute, and behind us I could hear the rhythmic tread of the Guards, closing up

20

in the rear. The others had already passed the gateway below, and I also was about to step into the court-yard when a touch on my elbow detained me, and I turned and saw a man standing at my side. I recognized him instantly as the Russian spy who had brought me the false information from Lina,—the same man who had dismounted at my gate from his bicycle.

" What do you wish ? " I asked, coldly.

" Pardon, Excelenz, but you are not liberated with the others."

" I am held as a prisoner ? " I asked, quietly.

" Yes,—for the present. Do not be alarmed, Excelenz ; doubtless freedom will come in time."

" Very well ! " said I, for I was so miserable that I really did not care what became of me.

I followed the fellow back along the passage, musing bitterly on my ruined hopes, too wretched and heart-sick to even notice where I was going. After a while I found myself in a little court, surrounded on all sides by the massive black walls of the fortress.

" Here is where prisoners are shot, Excelenz," observed the man.

I looked at the blank wall indifferently, and we passed on to a gateway which was guarded by a sentinel. Emerging from this, I found myself outside the exterior ramparts of the huge fortress, standing in a quiet shady lane, in which a droschsky was waiting.

" Enter, Excelenz!" murmured the man.

I stepped in without hesitation ; but, before the fellow could signal the driver to move, I stretched out my hand, and pointed at him, trembling.

" Tell your fellow spy that she was not merciful when she withheld the knife!" I cried, and sank back in the cushions, shaking from head to foot.

CHAPTER XVIII.

WHETHER the drive was long or short I did not know, but when at last the droschsky stopped, and a step sounded on the gravel beside the wheels, I unclosed my eyes and raised my head. A liveried servant stood bowing and fawning by the carriage step, evidently waiting for me to descend.   I did so listlessly, and looked around.   Before me lay a garden, bright with flowers and sun-warmed turf, high walled with fragrant hedges.   Among the blossoming trees and shrubs I could see the grey stone façade of a house, set back on the smoothly shaven lawn.

"Am I to go in?" I asked.

The servant bowed again, and asked leave to precede me.   I followed, glancing right and left, my sabre, which had been restored to me, trailing on the gravel walk, my sabre-tache swinging with every step. The flunky held the gate open, and I entered and followed him across the inner garden to the broad stone steps of the house.

Before I entered I looked with sudden suspicion at the servant, and asked him why I had been sent there. He replied very humbly that he did n't know, but that the house was ready for me, and he would pilot me to my own room.

"Do you know my name?" I asked.

He said that he did if I wished him to know it. His obsequiousness disgusted me, but, on second thoughts, I was not alarmed, because, I reflected, that if the Boznovian government wished to get rid of me it had had plenty of opportunity when I was in the Black Fortress. Still I had heard of traps, and assassinations are not uncommon in the Balkan States.

The room he led me to was a cheerful, sunny chamber on the ground floor, looking out upon the garden. Across the hallway I could see a dining-room with table set for two, and I asked him whether there was anybody else in the house. He replied that there was nobody there except myself and one servant.

"You are the servant?" I asked.

"Yes Excelenz."

"You are ordered to do my bidding?"

"If Excelenz permits."

"Then I bid you tell me where I am."

The servant was silent.

"Never mind then," I said, "but I should like to know why the table is prepared for two."

"Excelenz expects a guest?" asked the servant respectfully.

"Confound it, that's what I want to know," I said.

"If Excelenz permits," said this most extraordinary servant, "I will prepare the bath."

I was very glad of that and I told him to do so at once. In a few minutes he returned, and showed me through my bedroom into a spacious bath-room where a marble basin, sunk into the tiled floor, lay full of deliciously tepid water.

Everything was there in place—soap, towels, bath-robe, and, to my surprise, fresh underwear and linen. He took my uniform and boots away, shutting the door softly behind, and, without more ado, I stripped and plunged in. It was delicious after the hot, dusty days passed on the march. I splashed about, wondering whether I was to be assassinated like Marat in his bath, and not caring much anyway, provided my Charlotte Corday did her work well. For I was very miserable and tired of life, and when I drew on my bath-robe and the servant came to shave me, I felt that I had no right to enjoy the cool lather and grateful razor.

At last I was dressed again, my boots spotless, my uniform brushed and pressed.

"What are you going to do now?" I said, eyeing the servant.

"If Excelenz permits I will retire to prepare dinner. Luncheon is served in the garden."

"I want no luncheon," I replied, and walked out into the garden.

Everywhere the roses were in full bloom

and their scent troubled me, for I remembered my own rose garden in the Tiflix
valley where I had first seen Lina. At
the thought my face hardened and I flung
myself into a rustic bench, clenching my
hands. Faugh! A maid,—a servant
with a servant's code of honour. What
else could a man expect? Of course I
had lowered myself and had been bar-
tered, sold, duped, and tricked! Was
it for pay,—for the recompense that a
hired spy receives? Was it for love of
country,—a real patriotism? It might
have been the latter,—I trusted for my
own pride's sake that it was. Oh, she
had worked it cleverly, taking service
with the Dowager Duchess von Schwiggle, duping and flouting the Duchess and
her schemes under her Grace's own Teu-
tonic nose. Then also when the bicyclists
came, she had appeared, pretending that
she had not known anybody was there.
What signals had she exchanged with
them while I, innocent as a lamb, imagined I was craftier than Machiaveli
when I introduced her as my wife. Now

I caught the full significance of her sarcastic compliment to me on my cleverness. And the Russian who had been treed by the bear; he doubtless was in constant communication with her. I ground my teeth as I thought of the whole miserable business—of that blow in the face that she had given me and my swift infatuation and declaration.

And as I lay there musing, I remembered the walk in the woods and the bouquet of orange and white orchids that I had slipped into her belt. And I remembered her arms about my neck and her lips' swift touch on mine; and I felt the breath of the star-lit evening when we sat together in the meadow watching for signals, while the crickets sang and the scented breezes stirred the grasses.—

"Excelenz, pardon."

I started up, brushing the sudden mist from my eyes.

"What is it," I asked sharply.

"Pardon, it is already five o'clock."

"Impossible!" I said, "I have n't been asleep."

I looked at my watch.   It was exactly five.   I had been brooding there in the sunshine for four whole hours.

"Well," said I, "what of it?   I shall not dine until six."

"Pardon, Excelenz, I am permitted to announce that her Royal Highness the Princess Sylvia of Marmora will honour Excelenz with her presence at dinner, at half past six."

I was too astonished to answer, and waiting a moment, the servant bowed himself away.

"The devil!" thought I to myself, "am I to dine with Witch Sylvia?   Lord defend us, what mischief is coming now?"

More agitated than I imagined I could have been by any announcement, I walked nervously up and down the gravel path, brushing the roses with my sleeves as I passed, chewing a leaf stem and pondering. What could Witch Sylvia want of me? Was this another of her madcap adventures?   Probably she was coming to pump me about the Duchess or possibly to satisfy a curiosity concerning the per-

sonal appearance of a man who had stirred two Kings and a few Dukes to war.
What was she like? People said that she
was very beautiful. I remembered that
when Lina described her to me and spoke
of her blue eyes and black hair, I had said
that I preferred Lina's golden hair and
violet eyes. Ah! that was ended forever,
—ended in shame and disgrace.

A sound of hoofs from the road startled
me and I turned towards the hedge. A
single rider was advancing at a gallop
along the highway,—a woman mounted
upon a strong black horse. I saw the
lithe figure outlined against the sky, I saw
the horse gallop up to the gate and stop,
and then I saw the servant hurry out,
bowing and writhing with obsequiousness
as the rider sprang lightly to the ground.

Was this the princess,—unattended by
even a groom? I could not doubt it, for
the servant was uttering exclamations of
" Highness " and " Princess," and there
was that in the bearing and carriage of
the small patrician head that corroborated
him.

I let my hand fall to the hilt of my sabre, took off my hussar's busby, and walked straight down the path to meet the Princess, the dreaded, feared, admired Witch Sylvia.

Then I bowed low and stepped forward, raising my eyes, determined to bear myself easily and coolly, but what I said was "God have mercy!" and I turned faint and trembled, for I was looking into the eyes of Lina.

CHAPTER XIX.

THE strangest moments of my life were passing as I stood there in the garden path, rigid, speechless, clasping my busby with one hand, clutching my sabre hilt in the other. My senses rocked and reeled, my eyes blurred under her gaze; I no longer felt or heard, I only saw those clear eyes looking into mine.

At last, with a gesture of command, she stepped into the path to the right, and I followed. Twice, as we moved along in silence, I saw her strike a rosebud from its stalk with her riding-crop, and, scarce-knowing what I did, I, following, stooped and lifted the crushed blossoms from the ground.

There was an ivy-grown group of trees, encircling a fountain behind the house:

and here she paused and tossed her riding crop and gauntlets onto the turf.

My eyes met hers for an instant, then sought the ground where her whip and gloves were lying. And upon the back of one small gauntlet I saw, emblazoned in scarlet and gold, the tiny royal crest of Boznovia.

She seated herself upon a marble bench, touching the skirts of her habit indifferently. Under the hem of her habit glittered a single golden spur.

" What have you to say ? " she said, without looking up.

" Nothing," I replied. I wondered that I found my voice at all. A swift change passed across her face ; there came a flash of menace into her eyes and they deepened and darkled like the soft colours that slumber in the depths of clouds before a storm.

" I am the Princess Sylvia of Marmora and sister to the King," she said, " and I am not accustomed to justify myself to anybody. Yet now it is my pleasure to justify myself to you,—to you

a foreigner, who bring to my country
the curse of the sword ;—who ride into
my land at the head of a fierce mer-
cenary army to force upon my people
what my people have repudiated by force.
What is it to you that cottages are
burned and wretched peasants lose their
all ? What is it to you that a peaceful
people are harried like starving wolves ?
Do you know what war is ? Do you
care ? Do you think it is all helmets and
horses and gorgeous trappings ? Have
you ever seen a cannon wheel crush the
breast of a dying man ? Have you ever
seen your black shells rip a woman into
shreds of quivering flesh ? You who eat
and drink when you will, who have but to
speak, and satisfy your hunger, do you
know what starvation is ? Have you seen
a city full of tottering skeletons, scraping
the filth from gutter refuse to find a bone ?
That is war !"

She flung herself breathlessly upon the
marble seat.

" That is war !" she repeated, closing
her white teeth ; " filth, disease, cold, star-

vation, rags,—all these are but words to you,—but these words are only a longer way of saying 'war.'   And you bring war to me and to my people!   Why?   Have you a wrong to redress?   Have you a principle to vindicate?   Have you even a private grievance that needs the blood of the poor to heal?   Is this why you bring this monstrous curse upon my country,— upon me and my people?   Ah no!   It is because you have been refused by a woman and you merely wish to divert your mind.   It is excitement you are looking for,—and you decide you will find it in war."

Motionless, speechless, I stood before her.   My hand grew numb; I no longer felt the sabre hilt under my straining fingers.

" This, then, is my justification," she said, bitterly, "and I would do what I have done again and again,—all that I have done, yes, if it tore my heart from my breast !   What I have suffered I pass over.   It was my privilege to endure what I have endured and God was merciful beyond all understanding, for He threw you into my path,—and I used you to His eternal glory and praise. Through you,—in spite of you,—not one drop of blood has been shed, not one mother's heart broken, not one wife widowed. To-day your armed hordes are tramping back unscathed, with clean hands and hearts ; to-day your allied Kings and nobles are spurring homeward, contented each with his little profit. Can I ask more ?"

" No," I answered at last, and turned away with bent head. And, as I turned to go my way, a touch fell upon my arm and I raised my head.

She stood there, pale, tearful, both arms outstretched, barring my path ; then with a great sob she caught my hands in hers, drawing my arms around her, close, closer, until her wet cheeks were hidden on my breast. Thus did the Princess Sylvia of Marmora choose to justify herself in the eyes of the man she loved.

.   .   .   .   .

It was early evening and the sun still gilded the tree trunks and tinged the

placid pool of the fountain as we passed
too and fro among the thickets of the
little grove. We stepped slowly and
gravely as befitted two young people who
are on the point of electrifying Europe.
My arm clasped her lithe body; her
white hand lay over mine, holding it still
closer to her side. I had been telling her
exactly how I loved her, and, having
paused a moment to breathe, she told me,
very innocently, just how she loved me.
All the purity of her loyal heart, all the
deep passion, fierce and tender at the
same time,—all these were mine,—for me
alone. She spoke simply, with no thought
of shame or coquetry; and she was so
sweet, so winsome, turning to me with
questions and asking for advice and aid,
—she who had duped an army and two
Kings, — she who had held by sheer
strength a furious struggling trapped man !
Oh, I was very grave and serious when I
received her pretty " merci, mon cœur,"
as though she had been in direst peril. It
is right after all. A man must needs per-
suade himself that the woman he loves is

a little helpless and a trifle dependent. Otherwise he is troubled in his heart and sooner or later the devil intervenes.

Now there was one question that I had been aching to ask Lina,—I mean the Princess Sylvia,—but I dared not, being uncertain as to her reception of an observation which, after all, it was perhaps none of my business to offer.

She solved the problem herself, later, and this is how she did it.

"Do you like my hair?" said she, touching a dark curl and daintily bringing it under discipline.

That was just the trouble. The Lina that I knew had golden hair. I had sworn it was beautiful,—more beautiful than dark hair; but now, alas! Lina had suddenly become transformed into a lovely dark-haired Princess.

"If it's enchantment I give it up," said I dolefully.

She laughed, looking up into my face.

"The same eyes," I said, "but where —oh where, my Sylvia, is that twisted mesh of sunlight that you called hair?"

" It was a wig, goose."

Then, finding I was on safe ground, I swore by the nine gods that this dark silky head was the only beautiful head in the world, but she pretended to refuse all comfort and she wept for her blond disguise. " I don't see why," said I, "you ever wore it."

" The Duchess would have known me, and might have done me an injury."

"The devil !" said I.

" No, the Duchess," said Sylvia, gravely.

We strolled towards the house, I unwillingly withdrawing my arm, for Sylvia said that Max the servant might be indiscreet enough to look out of the window.

Dinner was announced, as she commanded, at once, and I had just time to run to my room and return to meet her and conduct her with most elaborate ceremony to her place.

At the beginning of the dinner we drank to each other in a light sunny-coloured wine out of glasses as thin as soap-bubbles. Sylvia ate three salted Ispha nuts

and then we found a philopena, which dis-
covery furnished us with most delightful
opportunities.

Once I remember how she held in her
delicate fingers a glass of the red wine of
Burgundy, and the candle-light shining
through, stained her white wrist crimson.

Now I do not suppose that many people would care to know just what we said
and did during that heavenly repast.   If
they do, they should not be indulged.

We said a number of things and we
looked a great many more, and we did
not eat enough to keep a canary-bird in
robust health.   I think Sylvia sipped part
of two small glasses of wine.   I was less
abstemious,—I took part of three.

She herself called for the silver lamp
and lighted a cigarette for me, then rose
and passed from the room, leaning lightly
on my arm.

A young moon was shining in the sky.
That it was there solely for our benefit
we never doubted.   Probably most lovers
can imagine what we did.   If they cannot
I decline to assist them.

"Sylvia," I whispered,—her face lay against mine, — "tell me about that bear."

"Casimir ?"

"No, the bear."

"That 's what I mean, my pet bear Casimir."

"Oh," said I, feeling that she was smiling, "so you really named him Casimir ?"

"Yes, but it was silly because Casimir is a lady-bear. Do you know what she did ? Only think, she ran away and had cubs all by herself."

A faint suspicion began to dawn in my mind.

"She ran away into the Tiflix valley from the Ezrox station, where they were transporting her by rail to Belgarde. She had been in the Zoo in Bazoum while the Exposition lasted."

"Hm ! So she had cubs in the Tiflix Valley ?"

"Yes,—and do you know she was so glad to see any one that when one of my spies stumbled across her she rushed for him and frightened him half to death. He went up a tree."

" Did he ?" I asked.

" Yes,—and do you know that Obadiah and the Duke of Babu who were out fishing were also frightened and ran up two more trees ?"

" I—er—I believe that Babu did mention it," I said carelessly.   " And you say the bear was—er—was not fierce ?"

"Casimir ?   Poor darling, she was delighted to see anybody."

" Not delighted at seeing a meal ?"

"Casimir ? She would n't bite a gnat !"

I was silent for a while.   Sylvia pressed her fragrant cheek against her clasped hands.

" Would n't bite eh ? " I asked again.

" No indeed."

" How did you know the bear treed Babu and Obadiah ? "

" Why my spy told me."

" Did he tell you anything else ?"   I asked suspiciously.

Sylvia was laughing softly and I rebelled and turned her face to mine.

"Stop it," I said, "how was I to know that the brute was n't an ordinary she-bear ?"

"I am not laughing," she said, "you were very brave and you did one of the cleverest things I ever heard of. Don't think I am trying to tease you; I only can't help remembering how mild and meek poor Casimir is and—"

"Oh Heavens !" I muttered, "to think that this tame bear should dog my footsteps and make an idiot of me in two countries."

It was Sylvia's turn to comfort me now and she did so until I also had to laugh.

For a few minutes we paced up and down the dusky garden paths under the young moon, too happy to think of anything but the present. I had drawn her arm through mine and I believe that we were saying to each other some things that would sound silly if repeated in cold blood, when suddenly Sylvia stopped short.

"What is it ?" I asked, taking quick alarm.

" Hush," she whispered, " walk quietly , with me ; do not offer to touch me,—see ! —see there ! Ah ! It is Prascoff ! He has gone !"

" Where, who ?" I stammered, staring out into the night. But she only repeated, " Oh, he has gone to the King ! What shall I do ! Oh, you must take me away with you ; take me now—take me away ! for my own spy, Prascoff, the Russian, has seen you kiss me, and it will go hard with me and harder with you if my brother the King confronts us."

The King ! In my great happiness I had forgotten that I was in love with the sister of a King.

" The King !" I said,—" your brother !"

" Are you afraid ?" she asked.

Then I laughed, and took her hand lightly in my own.

" No," said I ; " is there a horse here that I can ride ?"

" Yes ; in the stable behind the trees there are three. I have my own."

" Max !" I shouted, and a prompt voice came quavering : " Excelenz."

"Saddle the best horse at once!" I cried, "and saddle the horse of her Royal Highness."

Sylvia leaned heavily on my arm as I led her to the hedge gate, where we were to mount. In a few minutes the trample of hoofs came to us from the stable yard, and presently Max appeared, leading both horses. Quick as a flash I lifted Sylvia into her saddle, then sprang into my own.

"Max," I said, "we are going for a gallop."

The man was mute.

"Max," said Sylvia, "are you faithful to me?"

"Till death, my Princess," replied the servant, simply.

"Whither do we ride?" asked Sylvia. turning to me.

"To the nearest city and priest," I answered in a low voice.

"The nearest shelter,—and priest, are at schloss Lauterschnapps in Taximbourg."

"The Duchess' castle!"

"Yes; it is our only chance. The

other way leads to Tchatal-Dagh and Belgarde."

We were between the devil and the deep-sea.   I chose the devil.

" How far is Taximbourg ? "

" Forty miles."

" East ? "

" Yes."

" Va pour la Duchess ! " I cried ; " Max, we have ridden west,—if anybody wishes to know."

Max looked at Sylvia.

" We have ridden west," said Sylvia ; and we wheeled our horses sharply to the east and dashed out into the night.

CHAPTER XX.

A HEADLONG FLIGHT.

MY memories of that midnight ride
are vague, yet even now, as I
write, I can almost hear the night winds
rushing by, the creak and strain of saddle
and stirrup, the rhythm of hoofs in the
dark, galloping, galloping through woodland and valley, now sharp on the ringing
rocks, now dulled in the dirt, and now
again echoing steadily over the highway,
while the misty roadside bushes bent and
bowed in the flurry of wind at our horses'
flanks.

It was nearly dawn when we drew
bridle before the line of square painted
posts emblazoned with the royal arms of
Boznovia on one side, and the arms of
Taximbourg on the other. The frontier

at last ! Facing the highway stood a long low stone house, from which now appeared a sleepy soldier, trailing a rifle. He yawned and coughed, and asked us if we had anything to declare. We said that we had nothing dutiable, and he let us go, pocketing the gold piece I offered, and saluting my uniform, apparently as an afterthought.

"Is that a specimen of the Taximbourg soldier?" I asked, guiding my horse close to Sylvia's bridle-rein.

"Yes," she said, smiling, and settling her hair with one gloved hand; "do you wonder that King Theobald was not able to govern Boznovia when he proved incapable of ruling his own country?"

"Poor King," I murmured; "doubtless he is much happier to-day in his own home than he could ever have been in the Belgarde Palace."

"I hope he is," said Sylvia seriously; "I'm sure that I am." We both laughed at this, and I imagined that Sylvia saw no trace of the anxiety that was in my breast.

"Shall we gallop?" she asked; "the horses are not winded."

"Do you think we should gallop?" I replied.

"I think we had better," she said, leaning across her saddle; "we have done a very, very rash thing, my darling, and to-morrow all Europe will be ringing with it."

"Let it ring," said I stoutly;—"and perhaps, Sylvia, we had better gallop."

I thought to myself, "If it's going to ring, I'll give it sufficient to ring for."

Dawn was silvering the dew-tipped tree-tops as we shook out our bridles, and galloped on. The clean, fresh air grew sweet with the fragrance of unclosing blossoms; birds stirred in every hedge, twittering sleepily; a great sombre owl sailed from a crooked branch overhead, and floated away toward the darker forest depths. Along the road little pools of water grew pale and then pink as the east brightened, and, in the hush of early morning, a distant cock-crow came faintly to our ears.

Silently, close together, we flew along, our horses striding easily, manes, forelocks, and tails streaming straight out, flanks rising and falling without distress. And now, far ahead in the morning haze, a sweet bell tolled, and I heard a dog barking from the nearer hillside.

The solemn cattle stared at us as we passed through a farm-yard, the turkeys gobbled silly comments from their thistle patch, and a very small puppy rushed out at us, and chased us nearly a rod, barking until I feared for his tender throat.

Houses crowded along the roadside now, low grey cottages from the chimneys of which lazily curled the morning smoke. One or two heavy featured Taximbourgeois, carrying primitive scythes and wooden rakes, stepped aside to give us way, bidding us an apathetic "good morning!"

All at once a tower loomed up from the haze across the meadows,—a heavy, forbidding tower, squatty and unlovely.

" Schloss Lauterschnapps ! " panted Sylvia, " we are there ! "

At the same moment, the sun leaped from the forest, flooding the whole land with glittering gilded streams of light, and I saw, as by magic, a vast grey castle, close at hand, surrounded by trees and vineyards and red-roofed cottages, from which the morning vapours steamed and faded in the air.

By a common impulse we drew bridle,— the fortified causeway was close in front,— and we turned our heads and looked at each other.

"Suppose she drives us out," said Sylvia at last.

"She shall not!" I replied, setting my teeth ; but truth to tell I had little stomach for the work that lay before me.

"She is a dragon," said Sylvia faintly.

"No more than I 'm a Saint-George," said I.   Until Sylvia reads this she will never know how frightened I was.

"Don't anger her, will you, dearest ?" said Sylvia desperately.

"Good saints !" thought I, "what is this Duchess that even Witch Sylvia should fear her ?"   But I did not say

this aloud ; I merely observed that my sex
protected me, and Sylvia joined in my
very uncertain laughter.

"Come," said I, "it 's the devil or the
Duchess."

"I 'm a little afraid it 's both," said
Sylvia, but she gathered up her bridle and
trotted bravely across the dismantled fortified bridge, through the broad way that
led to the watch-towers and lowered draw-
bridge.

Straight up the stony street and under
the portcullis we rode, and then out again
into the castle court. Here, without waiting for my courage to ooze away, I sprang
to the ground, lifted Sylvia from her
saddle and, giving her my arm, walked
solemnly up to the high gate. There
was a bell rope hanging outside and I
supposed it was there to pull so I pulled
it. I regretted my haste a second later,
for a great iron bell began to clang and
bang, swinging and ringing aloft in some
steeple, filling the whole court with a most
hideously infernal clamor.

"I 've done it now," said I ; "if they

don't do something violent to us they deserve a place among the cherubim."

"It was the wrong bell," said Sylvia, holding tightly to my arm,—"oh here comes somebody,—and—he looks very angry !"

Somebody was coming,—coming at the top of his speed, saying rash unkind things at the top of his voice.

"You 're the porter, I fancy," said I, smiling ; "you see we are strangers and we pulled the wrong rope. We wish to see her Grace the Dowager Duchess von Schwiggle," I went on, ignoring his horrified protests and gestures, "and we wish to see her at once. Oh, it is very important, and I mean what I say, and you need n't make those queer faces, and it is useless to tell us that the whole castle is alarmed, because we know it, and it 's just as well that it is. Show us in,—yes, all those beautiful gold-pieces are for you,—show us in,—you 'd better take them !—show us in at once, if you please, and announce that we bring tidings of the army. Oh, you have tidings already ? And his

Majesty King Theobald is here?   What! their Graces of Taxil and Babu also? Dear me, how delightful.   Wake them all up and tell them that the Princess Sylvia of Marmora honours them with her presence.   You are losing time by gaping, my friend,—go quickly, and when you return, see that the horses are well rubbed and fed."

" Dear me," whispered Sylvia, " I never knew you could talk like that!"

" Pooh!" said I, " that is nothing ; wait until the Duchess comes."

We were now ushered into a long, gloomy room, heavy with indigestible baroc architecture, and we sat down, close together, upon a most uncomfortable lounge ; and there we waited.

" Pooh!" I repeated. " When the Duchess comes I will astonish and delight you, Sylvia."

" I hope you will delight the Duchess too," said Sylvia, moving nearer.

" Only wait," said I.

Alas, we had not long to wait.   Before I could get my eyes accustomed to the gloom of the vast chamber, a hastily-dressed flunky stalked into the room with an ultimatum from the Duchess.   Its purport was simply " go at once ! " but the leaden-eyed flunky clothed it in milder language.

" Go ? " said I, " not at all.   We propose to wait here until we see her Grace.   Kindly announce to her our inflexible purpose."

The flunky withdrew, agitated ; I saw other servants in the great hall, whispering in groups and stealing furtive peeps at us.

" The whole castle is aroused," said I ; " doubtless I pulled the alarm bell.   It sounded like a tocsin."

" I have been here very often," said Sylvia, " but you know that was four years ago,—before the Duchess was shocked at a little thing I did——"

" Hm !   I have heard about it, dearest."

Sylvia looked at me out of the corners of her eyes.

" I regret it now," she said humbly.

" I don't," I said, " my wife can do no wrong."

Then we sat silent, hand in hand, our eyes fixed on the outer hall.

"I was going to say," ventured Sylvia, "that when I was here I never noticed that bell-rope. It must be some recent horrid freak of her Grace."

"Never mind," said I, "if they don't conduct us to the Duchess I'll ring it again. I wonder whether Taxil is here. If he—Hello ! Who is this !—Why bless me it's Prince Saranitza ! "

I sprang up and took both his out-stretched hands in mine ; then, wondering, delighted, I presented him to Sylvia, who received him very sweetly because she saw he was my friend.

"Now what the mischief," laughed Saranitza, "do you mean by coming to unprotected castles at break of day and sounding the tocsin ? Why man, the castle's gone mad. Babu rushed out on the battlements crying, ' to arms ! to arms ! The Russians are upon us !' and Taxil is arming for the fray, and her Grace is racing about with Mops at her heels say-ing very funny things in a voice like a six gun battery."

Sylvia was laughing in spite of my horrified face, and Prince Saranitza, looking curiously from one to the other, twisted his blond mustache and stood up very straight.

"See here," said I, "if the Duchess won't receive us, can you not get a priest? On my honour, my dear fellow, two people never stood in sorer need of the offices of a holy man."

Saranitza was too well bred to show the slightest astonishment, but I do not think Sylvia would have blamed him if he had tottered.

"Do you wish a priest at once?" he asked soberly.

"Is such a marriage legal?" I asked Sylvia in a low voice.

"I don't know," she said faintly.

"But tell me, what is the law of Boznovia?" I urged.

"In Marmora it needs parents' consent and banns and civil and religious ceremony," she murmured. "I am of age and I have no parents living, but all the same the banns must be published three successive weeks in advance."

"Well, then we'll marry under the Boznovian law," said I. "Shall I ask Prince Saranitza?"

"Yes," she said, her face all rosy.

Saranitza listened without apparent emotion although what I told him must have made his aristocratic senses tremble in the balance.

"You know, of course, that an earthquake in London would excite less amazement than this," he said to me in a whisper.

"Yes,"—what of it?"

"Nothing, my dear fellow,—God bless you!" and he clasped me warmly to his breast. Then he laughed and begged Sylvia's permission to retire, and in a few moments he appeared with a kindly young priest who looked as though he had hastily donned his soutane and neglected to shave.

"Marry us, my father, in the speediest manner that is possible and consistent with the laws of the Church," I said, "for our case is desperate."

Sylvia stood up, pale and red by turns.

"If this is not legal in the eyes of the

Boznovian and the Marmorian law,—do you care?" I whispered.

"No, murmured Sylvia, "it is legal for us; what matters the rest?"

And so, Prince Saranitza as witness, the good priest made us man and wife. And after he had gone away and Saranitza had kissed Sylvia's little hand and had followed him, Sylvia went into a dim corner of the room and knelt down to pray.

"Law or no law, neither King nor Church shall part us now!" I thought. In America it was legal and once on board an Atlantic liner, little I cared whether the marriage was legal in Boznovia or in all Europe for that matter.

Sylvia was still on her knees and I stood silent by the great mirror, watching her with fast beating heart, when a heavy step fell upon the threshold and a heavier voice boomed through the apartment—

"Herr Je!"

It was the Duchess.

"Blessed be His Name," I said devoutly, and looked straight into the Duchess' stony eyes. Sylvia had risen from her knees, pallid, but holding her head high. The Duchess' eyes gleamed fury.

"Go!" she cried, but I stopped her with a gesture.

"Madame," said I, "we are going when we are ready. We ran away to get married and we have been married and we sought your schloss because we were in peril of capture from the King of Boznovia, my wife's brother."

For a second the Duchess gaped, rigid with astonishment; then the poor old Dowager utterly collapsed. She had hysterics, an awful condition to witness in such a woman,—it was as though a grenadier of the guard was throwing fits.

Sylvia and I did what we could for her; we placed her on the lounge where she alternately sobbed and grinned and hugged me and hugged Sylvia until my own senses reeled a bit, and I began to wonder how the affair would end. Poor old creature! Sylvia smoothed and arranged her curl-papers and tidied the red and green dressing gown, saying soft pretty things to her and drying her faded eyes. Mops came wheezing in and growled at me, but I forgave him and attempted to caress him, and got bitten for my pains.

After a while the Duchess signified her desire to go, and she went, leaning heavily on Sylvia, who sent back to me a long, loving glance as she passed out of the door.

Saranitza, who was perfectly aware of what had happened, strolled in and took my arm, leading me to his own apartment.

" You see," he said, " the old lady is all right now ; she kicks up an infernal fuss and says nasty things but, I tell you, a bold coup-d'état wins her every time. Why, man, she 'd defend this castle against twenty Ruperts now ! And she 'll do more ; she 'll see Bismarck.   He 's in Taximbourg this week to take the waters, and if she asks him he will smooth things over, and Europe wont say a blessed word."

" Europe may not, but what about King Rupert ? " I demanded.

" Rupert ?   Pooh !   He knows well enough that he only holds his throne down by the grace of God and Otto von Bismarck."

I flung myself on a lounge, completely exhausted, and looked wearily up at him.

"There is one thing, however, that I wont forgive you for," said Saranitza laughing down at me, " and that is that your confounded tocsin most hideously disturbed the slumbers of my fiancée."

" Is she here ?" I asked, incredulously.

"Here ? I should say so. I 've two months' leave to marry in, and as soon as her parents come from the Bosphorus we are going to Vienna to be married."

" Bosphorus !" I stammered.

"Yes, why you must have met her,—I declare I forgot that last night she said she knew you—"

"Marjory Grey !" I cried, sitting straight up, " oh I am glad, I am delighted !" and I laughed and hugged him and wrung his hand until he protested.

"Why I did n't know that you were so well acquainted," he said mildly, "my fiancée never told me about you till last evening—"

"We were boy and girl together," I said, radiant with happiness, "we were two youngsters who had a very jolly time as two youngsters can only in America. Is Grey Pasha going to bring his lovely wife to schloss Lauterschnapps? If he does, the three most beautiful women in Europe will be together under the same roof."

"And also the three happiest fellows in all the world," he smiled.

"Yes," said I, seriously.

Mops, passing the door, growled at me.

"He 's a German dog," said Saranitza, "his bite is worse than his growl. Let us be thankful that her Grace is only a Taximbourgeoise."

"I am," I said, earnestly.

Then a trumpet peal from the court brought us both to our feet.

"Sainte Vierge !" whispered Saranitza, "it 's Rupert of Boznovia !"

I stumbled to the window and looked out. In the court-yard below a trumpeter of the Boznovian cavalry sat on his sweating horse, and beside him, grey with dust, King Rupert towered in his saddle, brows knitted, eyes fixed on the porter's gate.

CHAPTER XXI.

I T took me but a moment to make up my mind. I picked up my busby, adjusted the golden-scaled strap firmly beneath my chin, snapped belt and sabre-tache under my dolman, and, picking up my sabre, hurried down the stairway and out into the court-yard.

The King paled a little when he saw me, and straightened up in his saddle, but his eyes sparkled with fury, and his hand flew to his sabre guard.

"That's what I want!" I said; "if you have any grievance against me, in Heaven's name let us settle it now!"

By all the laws of code and country the King was held to be incompetent and above the necessity of resenting personal insult, yet I knew I had not misjudged

349

the man, and it was the man, not the King
who replied haughtily, and sprang from
his saddle right at me, sabre glistening in
the sun.

Clash ! Crash ! rang our sabres in the
stony court, starting sharp echoes from
turret and archway ; and the startled
horses reared and snorted, neighing
shrilly as the trumpeter struggled and
backed, straining in his saddle.   The
King pressed me so furiously that I gave
ground, moving diagonally across the
court.   I saw the broad blade of his sabre
flashing and turning before my eyes, I
heard a shout, a warning cry, a trample
and snort, then something struck me and
I reeled and pitched forward, the sabre
falling from my nerveless hand.   I must
have lain unconscious for a moment or
two, for, when I struggled to rise, my
head was gently pressed back into two
soft arms !   I looked up.   Sylvia bent
above me, white and silent.   And now I
also saw the King, motionless, sabre
lowered, standing in front of me, but he
was not looking at me.   Beside him stood

an old man, dressed in ill-fitting snuff coloured clothes, the sleeves of which were
too long and fell over his withered hands.
Under his slouch hat his prominent pale
eyes flickered ; the deep lines in his square
jaw stretched along his cheek ; his mouth
tightened under his white moustache.

It was Bismarck.

"What is done cannot be undone," he
said, looking at King Rupert. "If the
Princess Sylvia has chosen to place herself outside the pale, the Princess Sylvia
must take the consequences.   But I will
have no scandal ; do you understand,
King Rupert? The Czar and I placed
you where you are for one purpose, peace.
I will not have the peace of Europe disturbed because of Boznovia. It is the
tinder-box that I most fear ; and when I
say that I fear it you will understand that
I am in earnest."

" The marriage is not legal," said King
Rupert hotly.

Bismarck smiled and bent his grim face
upon Sylvia, crouching beside me on the
pavement.

" Do you hear what your brother says, my child ? " he asked with a touch of malice in his smile.

" This is my husband," said Sylvia, holding my head to her breast.

Bismarck let his thin hand fall upon the head of a great dog that had walked up beside him.

" Well ? " he said, turning suddenly on King Rupert.

" Sylvia," said the King, " are you mad ! Will you put me to shame and scorn in the face of all Europe ? "

"You are shaming yourself," she said. " Go back to Belgarde and I will try to forgive you ; but if you lift a finger against my husband it will bode ill for Boznovia !"

I struggled again to rise but she held me back, calling on Prince Bismarck to keep her brother away from me.

Then the Duchess got hold of King Rupert and Bismarck walked on the other side, the great dog stalking at his heels. A thin stream of blood trickled into my eyes and down along my chin and Sylvia wiped it away, and held me closer.

I saw it was wisest to let things take their course so I said nothing more, and presently King Rupert and his diplomatic mentors passed out of the court through the castle gate.   Confused and weak as I was I pitied King Rupert with two such grim masters at his elbows.

At last Sylvia bent over me again, touching my forehead fearfully, and I smiled and answered the question in her eyes: "I am not hurt."   Did your brother cut me down?"

"God forbid!" sobbed Sylvia, "the trumpeter's horse backed into you and trampled you.   Oh my darling, your head is crushed and I am the most unhappy girl on earth!"

"Nonsense," said I, "it is merely a scratch.   Let me sit up, Sylvia.   There, see, I am all right; hello! here's Saranitza, and Marjory Grey!——"

Marjory came up to me and frankly took my hand in hers.

"You will need a half dozen stitches in that noddle of yours," said Saranitza cheerily, "come, lean on me, old fellow;

no bones broken ?   Cristi ! you were ridden down before I could make you understand.   It 's all right ; King Rupert will take Bismarck's view of the case and you need n't worry."

Sylvia supported me on one side, Saranitza and Marjory on the other, and we moved slowly up the steps and into the great dark chamber where the priest had made Sylvia and me man and wife.

" It 's a sorry ending to my military career," I said feebly ; " I understand now that I was never intended to wear sabres and spurs."

"Whatever you wear you honour !" said Sylvia gravely.

With her hand in mine, lying stretched on the lounge, I underwent the surgeon's examination and later a good deal of washing and stitching and odor of sickly smelling colodian.   The surgeon was an old man and not too gentle in his operation but I said nothing and watched Sylvia's tender eyes.

"Can he travel?" asked Saranitza, bending over me.

The surgeon said I could play leap-frog if I desired to but if I was prudent I would avoid such amusements.

"Old bear!" said Marjory, after the surgeon had taken his leave; "I wonder if you could stand the journey to the Tiflix valley.   Prince Bismarck says that the sooner you two rash young people leave Taximbourg the better it will be for all concerned."

"Then," said I, "let us go in Heaven's name, for this is not the sort of a honeymoon that I should have deliberately selected; should you, Sylvia?"

"No," said Sylvia blushing and smiling through her tears.

"There is a britzska waiting when you are ready," observed Saranitza; "Bismarck ordered it."

"Well," said I, "that seems to settle it," and I stumbled to my feet.

Babu and Taxil came in and greeted me warmly, promising to visit us at the shooting-box in the Tiflix valley.   Babu spoke vaguely of bear hunting but I held my peace, avoiding Sylvia's delighted eyes.

Marjory Grey and Prince Saranitza were very thoughtful and cordial. They made us as comfortable as possible in the britzska, wishing us all sorts of blessings and happiness, and bidding us God-speed in the name of the Dutchess who had gone to Belgarde with the unwilling but helpless King.

"Oh, never fear, she will visit you!" said King Theobald, coming in, clad in a rough suit with a leather apron tied around his waist.

"She will be welcome," said Sylvia sweetly.

The ex-King wagged his head and rubbed his blackened thumbs over his apron.

"She does n't know everything," he said; "she does n't know that I am ten million times happier here in Taximbourg playing blacksmith at my new forge than if I were yawning my life away in the Belgarde Palace, tormented by idiotic ministers."

"Ahem!" coughed Taxil.

"He rides but ill the horse he shoes so

well," murmured Saranitza in my ear; " bon chien chasse de race ? "

So at last we said good-bye, and the driver cracked his long lashed whip, and the britzka rolled away, followed by a storm of rice from Marjory Grey's mischievous hand, and one of Babu's spurred boots from the equally mischievous Saranitza.

I lay back in the britzka, weak, happy, holding my wife's white hands against my lips.

MOSTLY CONCERNING BEARS.

SYLVIA and I sat on a rustic bench in our rose garden, examining wedding presents and watching Obadiah and Casimir the bear.

The presents were heaped up in Sylvia's boudoir, nearly to the ceiling, and now this new batch had been brought by Constantine, and of course it was necessary to examine them at once. There was a golden tea-service from Marjory Grey, and a Persian coffee set from Prince Saranitza. The Duchess sent nearly a ton of hideous bric-a-brac, also a wretched dog of the breed of Mops. However, as long as he only snapped at other people, Sylvia and I decided to harbour him. King Theobald sent us half a dozen golden horse-shoes of his own forging, though

what he expected us to do with them I
was at a loss to understand, until Sylvia
tacked them over every door in the house.
Their Graces of Taxil and Babu united in
a gift of live-stock, nine drab-coloured cows
and a spotted pony. General Bombwitz
sent me a snuff box of depressing design,
and to Sylvia he gave a fan, so awful that
I presented it to Constantine's daughter,
who wept with delight at my munificence.
The King of Caucasia, Count Vladina,
General Brimborio, all of the general
staff, and the Duke of Etropolis, united
in a gift of silver plate that made me
giddy to contemplate. Clisson sent Sylvia
some rare old Caucasian wine, and to me
he presented a sabre and a sarcastic note
ending : " you and Napoleon differ somewhat as to tactics
mais—n'importe ? voici le sabre
                    le sabre
                    le sabre ! "

Sylvia was indignant, but I laughed a
good deal secretly, for I appreciated the
Grand Duchess of Gerolstein.

And so we sat there, examining, planning, glancing at the weird antics of Obadiah and the bear, who were apparently conversing together upon the lawn.

"I wonder what he 's teaching that bear now?" mused Sylvia, arranging a stray curl thoughtfully. The bear's nose was almost touching Obadiah's, and the latter stood with both hands upon Casimir's shoulders.

" Doan git gay, Mars Bear," said Obadiah, lifting a warning finger, "doan yo' git so brash an' pestiferous,—put in yo' tongue! Now,—now we is gwine dance de pea-vine! Lef' foot, right foot, lef' foot, right foot, shuffle!—hyah yo'! stop dat hoppin'! Hist yo' feet up like ole 'Diah! Lef' foot, right foot, lef' foot, right foot, mizzle to yo' pardner,—hyah! doan' yo' hyah, ole 'Diah say 'mizzle'!"

" Is that English?" asked Sylvia, laughing.

"You know well enough it is n't," I replied.   I had learned, not without some chagrin, that Sylvia spoke English as well as I did.

"Obadiah is paying poor Casimir for treeing him," I added, and I glanced askance at Sylvia.

The mellow evening light tinged the meadow pond where geese and ducks steered to and fro, craning their necks after the dancing gnats. Rose tinted clouds piled high over the Osman Peak, casting strange shadows across the notch below the cragged heights. From the garden came the metallic scream of the old silver pheasant, the babble of turkeys and the whinny of horses in the stable.

"Get me a rose," said Sylvia capriciously.

I brought her a great bunch of spicy Turkish roses. She placed them in her waist, humming a song as her white fingers lingered among the blossoms.

"These buds are sweeter," said I, holding out two dried rose-buds in my hand.

"Where do they come from?" asked Sylvia, looking up at me.

"You struck them from the bush with your riding-crop that afternoon,—don't you remember?"

" Poor little buds," she said, bending tenderly over them ; but it was my palm, not the buds, that her lips brushed.

Then she sprang up and seized me with both hands, pushing me before her through the garden.

" Come and walk with Casimir and me," she insisted ; " you do nothing but sit and smoke and snap gun-locks all day and it is not healthy ! Obadiah ! Go in and bring your pruning shears. Look at that hedge. Are you not mortified ? "

" Yessm," said Obadiah rolling his eyes.

" Dear me," sighed Sylvia, slipping her arm through mine, " I really do not know what would become of this valley if I were not here. Casimir ! Follow close ! Closer ! No,—you must n't shove your old nose in between my husband and me. I love you very much but——"

" But what," said I.

" Never mind," said Sylvia, with a faint smile.

So we walked away into the flowering woodland, where the rushing Tchiska made music for us and the orange and white orchids spread a carpet for us, and all the little birds chirped shrill evening hymns in praise of the loveliest woman in all the world, my wife, Witch Sylvia.

THE END.